THE DISTANT WHISPER

Kenneth C. Cancellara

AuthorHouse™ LLC
1663 Liberty Drive
Bloomington, IN 47403
www.authorhouse.com
Phone: 1-800-839-8640

Published by AuthorHouse 01/21/2014

ISBN: 978-1-4918-4824-1 (sc)
ISBN: 978-1-4918-4823-4 (hc)
ISBN: 978-1-4918-4822-7 (e)

Library of Congress Control Number: 2013923776

PROLOGUE

The small fishing boat far on the horizon slashed against the rough waters of the Tyrrhenian Sea like an unguided toy, as it desperately sought to aim itself toward the safety of the distant pier.

It was late Autumn in the southern Italian Province of Campania. The hordes of tourists who had made their seasonal pilgrimages on the Amalfi Coast had largely retreated. Once again the locals had vanquished their friendly German, French and British invaders and had regained control of their territory. Tranquility now again reigned over the small towns and villages dotting the Amalfi coastline from the southern part of Sorrento down to the Town of Amalfi itself.

Mark Gentile stood on the terrace of the small apartment he and his wife Marina had purchased earlier that year. It was a small home that had been built straight out of the rockface of Monte Comune and Monte Sant'Angelo on which Positano had been created from the edge of the water, up several hundred feet from the sea.

The terrace had the same breathtaking view of the Gulf as its neighbor, Le Sireneuse Hotel, as it hung vertiginously-suspended over the precipice. It had taken Mark a few weeks to perk up sufficient courage to peek over the edge of the open four-foot high steel barrier that separated safety from the deep waters below. Marina had not yet attempted to accost the banister although, with every passing week, her imperceptible advance toward it continued, inch by inch. The pristine and vivid hues of the sea as the eye lifted toward the horizon and the cornucopia of multi-colored autumn flowers and hanging baskets adorning every terrace overhanging the hills served for Marina an irresistible magnet pulling her, or so it seemed, closer and closer to the protected edge.

The town of Positano is straight out of a dream. For the 4,000 permanent Positanesi and for the many thousands of annual visitors, their beloved dream-like community continues to exist, impossibly defying gravity.

Particularly at dawn, when the hopeful rays of the sun tend to merge the azure waters on which Positano floats with the rose, peach and caramel colors of its residences, the sight is indescribably mesmerizing. The dream must be seen; it must be felt; it must be savored slowly, gently, without hurry. Engineering skills with architectural elegance and simplicity combine to create a setting that's easily visualized but impossible to duplicate, or even logically rationalize.

And yet, this proud community, on its vertical axis, has been the guardian and self-appointed protector of the islands of Li Galli far in the distant waters of the Mediterranean since before the Saracens were traveling up the coastline ransacking towns and abbeys in their path.

Fiercely proud Positano has stood thus for many centuries, the Lattari Mountains to its back and the Tyhrennian Sea at its feet, mid-point between its cousins Sorrento and Ravello around Capo Sottile toward Amalfi and around Punta Campanello toward Sorrento.

It is shamelessly sensual as it constantly parades its multi-colored feathers, particularly from April to October, when it senses the presence of the multitudes of its adoring disciples, both nationals and foreigners.

Positano has created such an aura of spirituality for its visitors that each one feels a deep and personal connection with it—as if his experience is an exclusive, direct and unexplainable gift emanating directly from The Almighty.

And thus, Positano with no substantial material or economic contributions to give, has continuously and constantly offered to a stressful world its fascinating and deep-seeded beauty and a ready access to a spiritual introspection that tend to soften the most hardened heart and mellow the most seasoned stoic.

It was in this near-impossible of places that Mark Gentile had sought to continue his own internal voyage, that had begun the previous year.

PART 1

CHAPTER 1

As the wind and rain increased their intensity, the floating toy appeared and disappeared seemingly swallowed by the angry waters of the sea, only to be regurgitated shortly thereafter.

Mark Gentile pulled his jacket collar tightly around his neck and watched with fascination the jousting between Man and Nature. Even with its random detours, the fishing vessel slowly advanced toward the protective sanctuary of the pier. It almost seemed as if Poseidon, supreme ruler of the sea, was relinquishing his vice-like grip on the toy-vessel, benevolently pointing his trident toward shore, so as to bestow a reward on the captain and his hardened crew for the courage they had shown in battling the tempest.

As the wind whipped across the consolidated Positano hills, Mark turned his back to the screaming sea and headed toward the terrace door. He had experienced a turbulent internal struggle earlier in the year, much like the struggle between man and the sea he had just witnessed. In the process, Mark had rediscovered his youthful idealism and his lost sense of spirituality. He had sought refuge in his native Italy seeking to restructure his life with a more moderated balance between his past innate ambition for success and his acceptance that unconditional altruism and a sense of spiritual sensitivity are a sufficient reward for one's actions. In brief, Mark had tried to redefine his own personal happiness and had attempted to do so by relinquishing his important executive roles within Santius, the company of which he had been chief executive for so many years—roles that had lifted him to the pinnacle of material and societal success, but that had left a chasm in his soul.

As Mark and Marina had later basked in the beauty of the Tuscan landscape—the land of the European Renaissance—he had felt his own internal *Rinascimento* beginning to take form in his soul.

Mark had felt at ease with his decision to let go of his old ties to the life for which he had so strenuously strived during so many years and through so many personal hardships. He knew, however, that after so many years of climbing the ladder of material successes, his personal spiritual odyssey was not over, that it would be an evolving and longer-term work in progress. And so, Mark alternated between supreme contentment in living through his courageous decision to so dramatically alter the course of his life, and a sense of despair that the existence he had lived for so many years was now being abandoned. This contradiction left Mark with a palpable unease that was inexplicable, that had an indefinable source and that seemed to permeate his entire being.

"Come inside, Mark", exhorted Marina, "you're shaking from the cold wind and the rain. I have brewed a pot of fresh espresso. A strong cup of coffee with a drop of Grappa will warm you up quickly."

As Mark entered the room through the terrace door held open by his wife, he knew that his trembling was not caused by the cold and stormy weather alone. Rather, it was caused principally by an instability sourced deep in his soul.

Although unable to clearly decipher his future path, Mark had the premonition that his life was again about to take an unplanned detour and that he would soon be again embarking upon unexpected destinations.

CHAPTER 2

It had become a daily ritual for Mark Gentile. Up at 6:00 in the morning, every morning, regardless of the weather. Out the front door of his *villetta* for some quick wall push-ups before beginning his slow warm-up jog.

Normally, by the time he rounded the corner and climbed the steep ladder-like *scalinatella* on to Via Cristoforo Colombo, beads of perspiration would begin forming on his brow. This was a signal to Mark that his body had warmed up sufficiently that he could safely pick up his pace. Left along Cristoforo Colombo, continuing up the hill as fast as he could, until his lungs were in oxygen debt, Mark's feet deftly hitting the flat cobblestones of the ancient street without ever landing in the troughs. Another left turn at the top of the hill would lead him down the scalinatella to Piazza dei Mulini, and keeping right, continuing at full speed down the stone staircase to the bottom of the hill to the coastline where, for a hundred meters, Mark would regain his breath and would stabilize his speed until his mind and his body, now totally in unison, commanded his feet to go seemingly on cruise control, effortlessly at ease.

It was during this flat stretch, sea to his right and Monte Sant'Angelo to his left, that Mark would allow his mind to wander off and recapture episodes of his past spiritual journey that had taken him from his executive tenure and ambitions in Toronto to his current life in his native land.

His mind active with these movie replays and his breathing hard but steady, Mark continued his run on the walkway toward *Le Rocce* (the Rocks) in the distance.

As he jogged, Mark often raised his hand to greet the fishermen back from a successful nocturnal catch, their boats bobbing in the sea with ropes holding them firmly to the pier.

Mark continued past *Bar Ristorante L'Incanto*, where the fishermen were headed to unload their pails full of seafood later to be converted for its daily patrons into a variety of seafood delicacies for the day's lunches and dinners.

Le Rocce was Mark's turn-around point where he would double back, pick up speed on the flat beach area until he reached *Le Tre Sorelle Ristorante*. Here, a quick right turn would force Mark to slow his pace as he now began to climb the staircase, the Tyrrhenian Sea at his back.

Mark wound his way up, past the attractive *La Tartara* clothing store, then left at the mural of the Virgin Mary of Positano, and then left again at the wall of Santa Maria Assunta and the San Vito mural.

By now, with Mark's knees succumbing to jabs of pain, his quadriceps would usually become wobbly with fatigue and feel like elastic bands. Strangely, though, even with his current reality clouded by pain and a state of semi-unconsciouness, Mark could dig deep in his mind and relive episodes of his past corporate experiences at Santius. He could recite by heart the eulogy at the funeral of his old mentor, Gordon Welsh: ". . . Gordon's most honorable trait was his sense of fairness and his moral fiber . . . whether watching a football game, heading corporate activities or dealing generally with life's vicissitudes, Gordon always believed it was important to succeed—but only if success came with fairness and integrity, otherwise, the price was too high". Mark had spoken from the heart, spontaneously and without a script. He had ended the eulogy by promising that these same principles of integrity would govern his own life both professionally and personally.

But had Mark, in fact, kept his promise to Gordon and to all those who heard that promise? More importantly, had he kept that promise to himself?

As the key questions kept ruminating in his mind, Mark never retrieved a satisfactory answer. Nevertheless, his mind seemed to automatically play and replay the same unanswered questions, and always without answers. As usual, this episode in Mark's past journey would be interrupted when, lactic acid having finally conquered his body, he would press the "pause" button just as he reached his front door, forty-five minutes later.

The movie reel would then be packed away in his mind, to be again accessed the next day and the next, when these past episodes would once more be vividly replayed in his mind's eye.

CHAPTER 3

"B*uon Giorno, Signora Gentile*", Giovanna greeted Marina as she and Mark entered the busy Bar Amarizio.

"*L'estate è ormai finita e i turisti sono scomparsi per un'altra stagione*— summer's over and the tourists have returned home once again".

"*Ciao Giovanna*. Yes, it's true. Peace and quiet are finally here again", answered Marina in a refrain that was being repeated often by the Positano locals.

As usual, it had been a busy five months for their town, and while every resident benefited financially from the arrival of these friendly invaders from all over Europe and the world, nevertheless, everyone—retailers included—invariably looked forward to recapturing their little corner of Paradise and enjoying it all for themselves for a few months in the off-season. It was now time for the Positanesi to begin their own relaxation and reflection. Time to recapture their cherished century-old customs. Time to reconnect with friends, abandoned during summer's frenetic pace. Time to be thankful for who they were and for the bounties—as modest as they may be—that God had given them.

These were a very spiritual people, Mark thought, a people who placed monetary gains in their proper perspective, far down life's main priorities of family, friends, thankfulness for their lot in life and the need to enjoy the simple and yet most essential pleasures life offered. For them, these included the daily *passeggiata* (after-dinner stroll) with their friends and neighbors and enjoying the beauty of their picturesque town that God had bestowed on them; a pleasure to be cherished today and to be preserved by them as custodians, in sacred trust, for future generations of Positanesi.

This chilly and damp November morning signalled the start of several months of spiritual awakening not only in Positano but all over the southern part of the Peninsula. The cafés would be invariably crowded and lively; the aroma of constantly-brewing espresso and freshly-baked delicacies wafting from every corner bakery and café on to the piazzas and streets; gentle or animated conversations with friends and neighbors would continue for hours until either the topic had been exhausted or until physical fatigue set in among its participants.

CHAPTER 4

It had become a custom for Mark and Marina to sit at a small table in the corner of the café, overlooking Piazza dei Mulini—normally, a small but bustling square in the centre of town.

But not this morning. The rain and fog had rolled in from the sea and had settled in the square much like an evicted squatter always escaping to a different location as if forced to do so by an entitled and unforgiving property owner. There was an eerie silence in the square, a calmness that seemed to signal the seasonal inactivity for which the Positanesi had been waiting.

Their silent reflection was interrupted by the melodic voice of affable Giovanna: "I have taken the liberty, with your permission, to bring your usual *doppio espresso macchiato*, extra dry for Marco and less so for Signora Marina", announced the proud owner of the café in a tone much more formal than the occasion warranted. "But this morning, I insist that you try a slice of our *torta di uva schiacciata*—a simple but delicious baked pie filled with local red grapes mashed by hand and drizzled with a sweet *limoncello liqueur* made from lemons grown up the road in

Piano di Sorrento". Giovanna's smile lit her establishment as she slowly pronounced every syllable ". . . baked pie filled with local red grapes . . . sweet *limoncello liqueur* . . .", with such gusto and such exaggerated body articulation that it seemed as if she were, at that very moment, herself carefully tasting every molecule of that deliciously-sounding concoction.

"This recipe has been handed down from generation to generation and now from my mother to me . . .", and then reading from her mental recipe, she continued ". . . it is simple and yet not so easy to make. You need just the right amount of water; the dough must be worked but not overworked; the grapes must be of an exact ripeness and of the right sweetness; the wood in the oven must have heated the bricks just to the right temperature . . . and, of course, the *limoncello* must be made by local artisans who have learned the art over centuries using lemons ripened by the Campania sun", she continued with a smile that showed both regional pride and personal satisfaction. And, of course, demonstrating that the recipe, far from being "simple" was almost impossible to duplicate.

Giovanna stopped and looked skyward as if searching for further descriptive inspiration. Noticing her struggle, Marina quickly came to her rescue and suggested: "We are certain that this will be heavenly. It looks delicious and I know we will absolutely enjoy it. *Grazie, Giovanna".*

But Giovanna wasn't quite finished, and as she placed the coffees and the generous pieces of the *torta* on the table, she half-turned away from her guests and concluded: "If you like it, you will make my mother very happy. But, if it's not perfect, I won't tell her as it will break her heart . . .". And before either Marina or Mark could give her their renewed reassurances, Giovanna hurried back toward the kitchen and with her right hand twirling in the air, added: "Either way, these pieces of *torta* are compliments of Giovanna".

Such was the generosity of these people, Mark thought. A wish to give to others without the expectation of anything in return. No thought of profit margins; no intention to "fatten the bottom line". For them, virtuosity lay precisely in the simple and genuine idea of sharing with neighbors whatever possessions they had the good fortune of having.

This was a simple yet profoundly difficult concept to grasp in a world that had become accustomed to striving for any advantage, individually and collectively; that expected, indeed demanded, value and preferably exaggerated value, for every personal act or omission; and that converted most activities into financial objectives and results.

CHAPTER 5

The rain and the wind had picked up, but although physically still at bar Amarizio, Mark was no longer a witness to the events both inside the cafe and in the piazza. He had been transported to another time and place; a time when generosity of spirit was the predominant criterion that judged one's virtue or lack thereof. Mark was now Marco again over half a century ago when his grandfather's open arms and his smile were all the reward Marco had sought or needed from his daily ambitions. At that early age, Marco had never sought, or aimed for, external rewards. His grandfather's benevolent reception; his hugs and his approving words and encouragement were all that Marco had needed to be happy.

In the last few months, as he had attempted to reconnect with the spiritual side of his life that had for so long remained dormant in his soul, Mark had often philosophized on one's journey through life with reference to his own spiritual odyssey. This work in progress, as Mark preferred to describe it, had become a consuming obsession for him from the moment his decision to remain in Italy was made by him and Marina as they had become enchanted with the beauty of the Tuscan landscape, several months earlier.

Mark's thoughts were now interrupted by new activities outside. He sipped his espresso macchiato and felt the foamy liquid immediately re-energize his senses. At that moment, the bus from Sorrento stopped in front of the cafe, and the piazza magically transformed itself into a circus of events. Children either dragged or carried by their fretting parents as they descended from the buses and shielded themselves from the driving rain; passengers waiting for their baggage to be taken out of the vehicle's womb; departing persons haphazardly queuing for entry into the bus, impatiently waiting until the last of the arrivals had descended.

CHAPTER 6

As the scene in the piazza continued to unfold, from the corner of one eye, Mark could see Marina's lips moving, but as if in a trance, he couldn't hear a word. Rather, Mark dusted off from the deep recesses of his mind a movie documentary that had been made half a century earlier and clicked the "start button".

"*Alzati—Marco. E tardi. Tuo nonno ti aspetta*—get up, Marco. It's late. Your grandfather is waiting for you", Mark's mother whispered as she gently shook the small boy from sleep, early one morning.

It was dawn in his hometown of Acerenza and already one could hear the clapping of hooves on the thousand-year-old cobblestones below. Marco had so trained his ears from his grandfather's varied lessons in life, as his nonno called them, that, merely from the noise of the hooves, he could pick out a horse from a mule from a donkey. In fact, Marco often shrieked with delight when he actually identified a specific animal and owner and would proudly announce to his smiling grandfather: "*è l'asino di Patrizio Cevalo . . .*—it's Patrizio Cevalo's donkey-*"* and, to confirm his verdict, he would run to the door to exclaim victoriously "*Ciao, Patrizio. Buona giornata*".

Today, Marco and his grandfather would be travelling, as business partners, to the neighboring town of Pietragalla for some important transactions. The harvest seasons would soon arrive and farm workers would be needed to help out with the tasks. Although the nearby town was only twenty kilometres away as the crow flies, the journey there would be arduous and would take several hours. Most of the towns and villages in Mark's native province of Basilicata had originally been created as hilltop fortifications with massive stone walls to serve as protection, at first from invading foreigners and, much later, from bands of marauding thieves who would travel from town to town to steal and pillage. These towns sat in isolation at the very top of every hill in the southern string of mountains forming the Apennines—that metaphorical spinal cord that held together the upper body of the Peninsula with its lower part.

Marco recalled vividly his childhood experiences when, at twilight, he and his friends, Luca and Gianni, would often sit high on the walls at Acerenza's Gate of San Canio staring out in the distance as the twinkling lights of the nearby towns would appear and disappear in the darkness. As day turned to night, the various clusters of lights dotting the landscape transported Marco into a magical world of astronomy where he would visit each town—each world in a different galaxy—to find imaginary action and adventure.

CHAPTER 7

The movie documentary continued for Mark.

Their mule packed and ready to go, Marco and his grandfather set out for the day—long journey for Pietragalla. Down the side of the mountain they would start, winding their way to the lazy Bradano River below.

The first segment of the trip was the easy part. The climb of almost a thousand metres straight up to the top to Pietragalla was infinitely more difficult. The narrow path was rocky and beast and man labored mightily in their slow and methodical advance. But Marco, precociously fit from his daily runs from the centre of Acerenza to the family farm Alvanello, routinely sprinted ahead, at once encouraging his grandfather and Peppino, their mule, to follow more quickly in his footsteps. Marco's early ambition to win, to stay ahead of the crowd, was already forming and exhibiting itself, even at that early age. It would be a character trait that, much later in life, adult-Mark would have difficulty abandoning.

At one point during the voyage, as the sun started its morning voyage from the distant Adriatic Sea and over the mountains, Marco's grandfather stopped Peppino and quickly disappeared behind a line of trees along the side of the path. A few minutes later, he re-appeared grasping two large peaches and a smile that seemed to say: "the hunt for breakfast went well this morning". Nonno spread a small blanket down on a large rock and laid out the *colazione*—the morning breakfast of freshly-picked peaches, crusty homemade bread baked the day before by Marco's mother, and cherry jam that had been lovingly made by Marco's grandmother just a few weeks back. A simple but delicious meal, partially made from home ingredients and partially derived a few minutes earlier from the "communal" peach orchard Marco's grandfather had accessed.

And, in this way, the two journeymen, separated by over half a century of experiences but wholly unified in resolve, ate and laughed as Marco wondered out loud how his grandfather had made the ripened peaches magically appear at precisely the moment of need, although Marco's smile likely betrayed his personal suspicions of his nonno's unauthorized harvest and his intention to go along with his grandfather's benevolent game of make-belief.

It was just before noon when they reached the centre of the small hill-top town. Marco's grandfather was now all business. The small town piazza was bustling with groups of men engaged in animated discussion. Marco followed his grandfather closely as he went from group to group, talking, laughing, shaking hands and mingling with the assembled groups.

Within an hour, their business had been done and they settled themselves down for their lunch which had been packed by Marco's grandmother earlier that morning: ricotta kept fresh by several layers of lettuce leaves, mixed with sugar to serve as a delicious spread on slices of focaccia. After lunch, as was *nonno*'s custom, a special treat for Marco: a mixed chocolate and lemon gelato from the local café.

Shortly after lunch, the two adventurers would set out again on their return voyage back to Acerenza.

Those were heady days for seven-year old Marco. Days of adventure and fun. As well, days of learning the importance of ambition and of integrity. His grandfather would confide in his young business partner on their way back: "Marco, never forget that when you deal with people, you have to be fair", he would caution, gesticulating with his right index finger.

His grandfather would explain how he had completed business at Pietragalla. He had hired half a dozen workers both to harvest the wheat and later in the season to return for the harvest of the grapes—*la vendemmia*. An agreement on the daily wages for the workers had been easily struck. This had been a good growing season for the area, and so, Marco's grandfather could be somewhat more generous with the wages. It was something well-understood by both "employees" and "management". No need to press the issue. No need for posturing. With both sides opting to be reasonable and realistic, a bargain would unfailingly be reached quickly, without acrimony and without fail. Personal pride in being fair to one another would preclude unjust and unrealistic demands or expectations. Code of personal ethics would allow for, and indeed would demand, a resolution that would have no winner, and importantly, no loser.

While Marco's young age did not fully allow him to understand all the intricacies of the notion of "fair bargain" that his grandfather was explaining and demonstrating by deed, nevertheless, even in his early youth, Marco's character was being unconsciously shaped so as to recognize the importance of acting fairly and equitably not through compulsion but out of principled fairness; from the notion that one should act equitably simply and exclusively because it was the right thing to do.

CHAPTER 8

As Marco-turned-Mark entered the world of business many years later in his adopted homeland of Canada, his grandfather's lessons from early childhood, although deeply engrained in Mark's character, were nevertheless forced to be parked in the deep recesses of his mind. Profit at all costs became the Machiavellian mantra for success. Indeed, profit was the only objective of any company that wanted to survive in a world driven by competition and materialism and the absolute need to succeed financially. Nevertheless, as Mark matured both in years and in his executive roles, an urgent sense of ethical resurgence began to pervade his mind. The lessons learned from Mark's grandfather began to surface and to guide both his business decisions and his personal life.

With increasing frequency, Mark came to realize that success without ethics and integrity was no success at all and that profit could be achieved through a careful weighing of activities that would lead to the desired result without misleading and without trampling over others who did not share the same point of view. And most important, without shaming one from looking at oneself in the mirror and approving the image he saw.

"*Non ti piace, Marco*?—didn't you like it—" Giovanna pulled Mark away from his reflections, as she saw that Mark's slice of *torta* had remained untouched. Marina looked at Giovanna as if to say "Mark is just now returning from one of his long and exhaustive spiritual voyages . . .". Instead, Marina replied: "Giovanna, Mark is a *chiacchierone*—a gossiper—and now that he's finished talking, I know that he will enjoy the *torta* as much as I have. You'll have to tell your Mom this was the most delicious *torta* I have ever tasted", added Marina both because she had wanted Giovanna to carry the message to please her mother, but also because she had meant it.

Marina had often seen her husband deep in thought like this and had grown to realize that, during such times, it was best to allow him the time and the space to complete his mental wanderings. Strangely, she didn't feel excluded from these voyages. Forty years of partnership had taught her to look deep into Mark's often distant eyes and feel as if she were accompanying him on his journeys. She had learned she could share with her husband his internal triumphs and also his numerous detours. Marina knew that Mark had always been a thoughtful person who often lapsed into self-analysis and philosophical meanderings. In fact, this was precisely the characteristics that had endeared him to her in their early university days. However, she had recently noticed that Mark's spiritual journeys had increased both in duration and intensity since their arrival in Italy.

Marina could see that Mark's permanence in his native land had caused an awakening of his youthful memories that were unlocking, from deep within, fundamental principles that Mark wanted to adopt to govern his new life.

CHAPTER 9

The early evening sea breeze lifting up the side of the hill was deliciously intoxicating. Marina sat on the terrace overlooking the tranquil waters below. The only movements were the gentle tide lapping against the long wooden pier and the resulting bobbing of the small fishing crafts safely anchored for the night.

Marina, sketch pad and pen in hand, did her best to capture the indescribable scenes around her and below. Every attempt, though, was met with nature's resistance—as if the scenes had been subject to some copyright protection that prevented mere mortals from recreating them.

The sky overhead and far in the distance had been painted like Renaissance frescos—vivid, suggesting, varied, and forever chameleon-like from moment to moment. Marina paused and put her pad to the side as she became one with the wonder that was God's gift to man. Even as an amateur artist, she knew that this blessing needed to be felt, admired and respected, rather than duplicated. No artist, no matter how masterful, could ever compete with nature in replicating this one-of-a-kind masterpiece. At that moment, Marina's eyes lifted upwards and followed the path of a seagull swirling effortlessly and gracefully in the limpid sky seemingly drawing a curtain over this priceless painting so as to preserve it overnight until the art exhibit would again reopen its doors the next day.

Marina had settled well in Southern Italy. Her days were fulfilling and happy. In the few short months since their permanent move overseas, Marina had perfected her Italian to the point where she could communicate freely on almost any topic. Her Italian studies in university many decades earlier and her continuing language lessons for many years thereafter were now paying their dividends. Mark did his part as well by purposely speaking Italian with her at home: "*Devi pensare in Italiano*—you need to think in Italian"—he would caution his spouse, "and not simply translate your thoughts from English". Marina and Mark had totally immersed themselves in the daily customs of this active and passionate region of Southern Italy.

In the morning, they would often walk over to Giovanna's cafe, where they had their usual *colazione* of a steaming cappuccino and freshly-baked chocolate *cornetti.*

The morning rite of cappuccino at their favorite cafe was, for Italians, an excuse—a delicious excuse—to catch up on news and gossip around town and around the world. The articulation of passionately-held views on politics, soccer or generally the art of living was a daily obsession for the local residents. It was during these debates that the true character of Italians came through. Eloquence was at its highest; unscripted debates, submissions and rebuttals were undertaken with gusto and determination. Every participant was, it seemed, a trained and passionate advocate. Improvised arguments rolled off the tongue and were presented as if meticulously prepared, reviewed and finalized weeks earlier.

Mark was often incredulous at the depth of the discussions and the gusto with which they were presented. Italians were at their best when given an opportunity to put on a show. They unfailingly raised the level of eloquent oratory, often aided by hand gesticulation and by dramatic facial expressions and body language. Indeed, the visual side of the personal submissions was so vividly presented that the oral accompaniment was often redundant. However, when the audio and the visual were merged, the experience was exhilarating and inspiring, for participants and spectators alike.

Mark and Marina would, at times, linger for hours, caught up in these continuing and meandering debates and waiting to see how these concocted stories would end. But they never quite ended permanently; they were merely interrupted, to be resumed the next hour, or the next day. There was never a loser. It was essential that every main protagonist feel that he had persuasively advanced his arguments regardless of the merit of the substance. Form was substance here, and form defined character. There was no hurry either for the presenters or for the spectators to draw the debate to closure. Indeed, after an intermission of one hour or several hours or several days, the debates would be rekindled, sometimes by the same, now-reenergized, actors and at other times by new participants.

There was never a shortage of volunteer-combatants. There had never been an instance that Mark recalled when Bar Amarizio didn't have any number of "Marc Anthony's" ready to show off their passions through improvised oratorical skills.

This delicious life-drama, acted upon by professional volunteers, was played out for all to witness and for the relatively inexpensive price of a cappuccino, or two.

CHAPTER 10

During their stay in Positano, Mark and Marina became fascinated not only with the present Italy, its people, its culture and its customs but also with its cultural inheritances over the centuries. They felt they needed to know, to discover, how this part of the Peninsula had developed over time. They began their investigation with a day trip to Pompeii.

The existence of Pompeii and the lessons it devolved to subsequent generations were topics of significant interest to these two eager adventurers. As students, many decades earlier, they had studied with fascination the development of the Pompeian society as a past example of ancient progress and well-being.

They decided that, today, they would be exploring Pompeii to experience the fascinating history of a people who lived and loved but, sadly, who no longer were.

Many centuries have now elapsed since ancient Pompeii was a living, breathing and active community, spread out on the sides of Mount Vesuvius. These original Vesuviani—as the residents of the current Town of Pompeii and its neighbors were called—had been industrious and fun-loving people who enjoyed the simplicities of life and the tightly-held bond to their families and friends. In this way, they carried out their daily vicissitudes in a corner of the world blessed with beauty, bounty and an attitude to live life to its fullest.

Tragically, it all ended quickly and without warning when an entire community disappeared in a flash on the morning of August 23, 79 A.D. The only traces of its vibrancy are now historical remnants that archaeologists have studied for years so as to give the world generally, and dedicated students of archaeology specifically, a detailed picture of the life of the Vesuviani.

Regrettably, the world's current participation in the activities of that indelible community of 20,000 inhabitants is now confined to walks along excavated streets and piazzas in the company of tourist guides from Naples who, as only *Napoletani* can, employ their considerable charm and passion to depict life as it was, or at least, as subjectively extrapolated and personalized by them through their innumerable recountings.

At present, Pompeii is but a tombstone for an entire civilization that has remained intact through petrification. Its streets, excavated out of dust and lava, are silent except for the words of reverence repeated by its over two million visitors annually. It is a place where one imagines; where one feels the sound of cymbals, the clapping of hoofs and the grinding of the steel chariot wheels against the tracks etched in the cobblestones carved through the years from their continual cutting.

Pompeii also evokes religious connotations. The *Santuario della Madonna*, was built on its grounds more recently in the 19th century. To southern Italians, this Basilica is the holiest of religious sites, where *Napoletani* and others come in droves to make offerings, take vows or have their new cars, from a modest Fiat to an ostentatious Lamborghini, blessed by the "men of the cloth" before they are launched like missiles on the Campania highways, roads and sidewalks for their continuous assaults on other vehicles and unsuspecting pedestrians alike.

For Italians, Pompeii is a reflection of the present-day contradiction between faith and consumerism, a contradiction felt throughout southern Italy. It is seen as representing the delicate balance between this gulf—a gulf with which, to this very day, the modern town of Pompeii, as well as the entire region, continue to struggle.

CHAPTER 11

Early one late November morning, Marina and Mark loaded their small Fiat with a *cestino* of freshly-baked bread and *pecorino* cheese, locally-grown dried peaches and figs and a bottle of *Aglianico del Vulture* and aimed the small vehicle twenty miles southwest along the coast and then fifteen miles north toward Sorrento.

The Amalfi Coastline has, perhaps, the most celebrated stretch of highway in the world. It twists and turns, hugging the precipice often several hundred feet from the rocky shores of the Tyrrhenian Sea. The waters, in a multitude of turquoise shades, unrelentlessly dance far below on massive protruding rocks. Every advance by the sea toward the cliffs is met with firm resistance by the rocks followed by the waters' hasty retreat. It is always a stalemate between two equally potent forces of nature: the sea, active and energetic in its repeated assaults, and the rocky cliffs, firm in their resolve to resist them. And thus, these unyielding forces have formed an uneasy but amiable coexistence, from time immemorial.

As Mark watched this continuous but unresolved struggle, he couldn't help but associate it metaphorically with his own internal struggle between the forces of ambition led by his calculated mind and the equally formidable forces of spirituality led by his soul. It was an open question, Mark thought, whether these could co-exist or whether there would be an inevitable collision between them that would result in his becoming a more fractured person. This was a fomenting battle that needed to be played out. There could be no shortcuts and no prematurely-declared winner.

As the sun furthered its journey from the Adriatic Sea in the east over the Apennines toward the western shores, Mark turned inland from the highway and guided his Italian chariot through the scenic but perilous road until it reached a flat meadow half-way up the steep cliff. It was now time to rest, to feed the stomach and to reenergize the soul.

Marina laid out their simple but delicious lunch on a flat rock and, as they nibbled on their cheese, crusty bread and dried fruit, Mark and Marina, their backs to the cliff, stared out below and far away toward the blue horizon. "It's as if diamonds were being sprinkled on the waters", began Marina gesturing out to the sea. Indeed, the sun's rays at this time of year carried a purity and a mellowness not duplicated in any other season. As the rays dug deep into the gentle rolls of the waves, it was as if a thousand prisms were refracting light over the waters simultaneously in all directions. It was a sight that was best left for quiet reflection rather than attempted detailed description.

Mark was lost in his reverie. "Personal happiness is the filling of one's soul with a sense of spirituality", Mark whispered to the quiet and seemingly attentive surroundings, "a feeling based not on external achievements, but on internal satisfaction", he continued. "It is only with one's feeding of the soul that lasting personal contentment is possible. All else, including material objectives—and, perhaps, particularly those—are merely temporary and passing rewards that eventually leave a void rather than filling it".

Marina looked at her husband lovingly and immediately understood that the time had again arrived to let Mark travel with his mind to destinations that would allow him to find peace and comfort in his soul.

In fact, over the last few months, Marina had learned to accompany Mark in his spiritual travels and to vicariously experience his internal turmoils, and his travels to imaginary, faraway places. Marina enjoyed the satisfaction of reaching with her husband his state of peaceful contentment. She comforted him when the final destination, or detours before reaching it, created for him turbulence and unease.

As hard as it tried, the sun had lost much of its early seasonal strength. Its rays, still bright but now more mellow, caressed rather than punished. Its energy was more controlled, more disciplined, more mature, less provoking. Its daily path was now a more accelerated voyage—in ways similar to man's path of life: full of promise at the start, intense and challenging at its peak, and more understanding as it approached the horizon of its journey.

"The only lasting reward in life that's truly fulfilling comes from within", Mark again whispered to Marina, as their gaze never wavered from the natural beauty that lay in the shimmering waters below. He continued, "personal ambition and the external rewards it engenders are addictive but, in reality, are merely transitory and do not provide permanent nourishment to one's spiritual needs", Mark affirmed in his low whisper. Marina placed her hand over his and retorted approvingly: "Of course, man also has the need to strive, to play out his ambition to succeed and his desire to engage in a quest that results in risk and reward".

These last comments shook Mark from his state of self-absorption. "Yes, but that is precisely what occurred in my own experiences as I began travelling down my career path. I became so absorbed in my personal wish to succeed that, like an addiction, my ambition became an absolute need to win, to reach the pinnacle. Before I realized what was happening, this initial benign ambition was being transformed into a Macchiavellian mandate not simply to succeed but to win at all costs. The end justified the means. The end was what mattered".

Marina had repeatedly seen Mark's critical self-analysis following his departure from the executive tenure he had held. At first, she had opted not to interfere, to simply allow him the time to reach his own conclusions. More and more, though, as her husband's emotional struggles continued to simmer seemingly without resolution, Marina became somewhat more participatory.

"Mark, we are beings with human emotions and, therefore, human frailties. You are not an exception, I'm afraid. You did what you were taught to do by the society in which we live. You strived for excellence as a student, as an attorney and as an executive. You did so not only to satisfy your own personal ambitions but also to care for the needs of your family. You've been a wonderful husband, father and soul-mate". Marina hesitated as her eyes welled up and her voice haltingly trailed off. "But, in the end, you were true to your principles and to your high sense of morality. To your credit, as soon as you concluded that your ethics were being compromised, you showed the courage to abandon thirty-five years of career plans in favor of the more balanced and more ethical lifestyle that you have adopted".

As the cantata of cicadas around them rose to a mellifluous crescendo in the autumn air, Marina rested her head lovingly on her husband's shoulder, tears of understanding gently following the contours of her lovely cheeks.

It was time for their physical voyage to continue. Sorrento, the northern gateway to the Amalfi coastline, lay just ahead. In a short while, they would reach Naples where they would meet their friends Luca Moranni and his wife Anna from Acerenza. They looked forward to spending time with them catching up on news from Mark's home town and discussing with Luca Santiana-Vino's financial results from *La Vendemmia*—the autumn grape harvest.

"If we leave now, there will be plenty of time for a late afternoon glass of *limoncello* in Sorrento before we're caught in the frenetic pace of Naples," Mark suggested as they packed away the remnants of their lunch and headed for their car.

CHAPTER 12

For several millennia, the Region of Campania has been a target for possession by numerous invaders.

It is a complex history dominated by wars and alternative dominance of the area by the Greeks, Etruscans, Sannites, and by the Romans to mention only a few. Even its neighbors, the Lucanians, Mark's provincial ancestors from the Province of Basilicata (formerly known as Lucania), were beckoned by Campania's fertile lands and advanced westward toward the Tyhrennian Sea. In their path, they settled in the fertile plains of Posidonia, later called Paestum in Capania, more than 2,500 years earlier.

Napoli—Naples—is the jewel, the centrepiece of this diverse region. Present-day Naples is a contradiction that often brings out the best and the worst in human nature. It is the city of the Neapolitan love song, the city where love and passion boil to seismic climaxes everywhere and at all times. The place where the Neapolitan woman is sanctified by her forlorn suitor; where jealousy reigns supreme; where entire love stories are habitually turned into poetic ballads and passionate lyrics. All is devoted to the common objective of satisfying one's innate need for *l'amore*—love. Not simple love, but passionate, uncompromising and guttural love that strips away logic and abandons common sense. Love that's founded on the twin emotions of impulsiveness and passion, the merger of which spawns an electricity that can lead either to uncontrollable happiness or, in appropriate circumstances, to depressive despair.

Through this tortured and, at times, bellicose history, present-day *Napoletani* have inherited a pugnacity; a loyalty to, and love for, their city; a perseverance no matter the odds; and a passion for *oggi*—today—that are unrivalled in Europe, and perhaps the world.

Neapolitans are, at once friendly, mischievous, fun-loving, non-committal, bent on making a living any way they can and generous to a fault. They are a sensitive, impulsive, highly emotional and aggressive people—characteristics that, depending on the circumstances, either garner respect and friendship or bestow benign fear . . . the kind of fear that tickles the soul, that keeps one vigilant but, at the same time, fear that allows one to proceed undaunted.

In brief, just like their long history of invaders, they are an unpredictable, contradictory and complex people who live their lives for the moment and whose decisions are usually dictated by the impulsive vagaries of the heart rather than by the cold and premeditated logic of the mind. Neapolitans are passionate, interesting and amiable Epicureans. They populate a city that's a mirror of themselves, a city that's vibrant, beautiful, mysterious, but a touch dangerous.

Together all these elements merge into the oft-cited Neapolitan refrain: "See Naples and then die".

CHAPTER 13

Mark reached the outskirts of Naples in the early evening.

As the Fiat rounded a corner on to Piazza Garibaldi, Marina rolled down her car window and they were immediately enveloped by a cacophony of sound and an intoxicating infusion of aromas.

It was Friday evening and the *Napoletani* were out in full force enjoying the last vestiges of late Autumn's mild weather. Young and old strolling around the Piazza, seemingly unaware of the Vespa motorcycles buzzing around them at full speed, equally on the road and trespassing on the sidewalks, with reckless abandon. "It's the miracle of coexistence and tolerance between man and machine", marvelled Marina as the controlled chaos unravelled in all directions.

They observed throngs of people, gelato in one hand, the other entwined into a friend's arm—males or females indiscriminately—laughing, talking, gesticulating. Young and old enjoying one another's company, parading themselves in this most ritualistic of all Italian customs: the evening stroll, *la passeggiata*.

The aromas of freshly-baked cannoli and sfogliatelle pastries, freshly-brewed espresso, *limoncello* and waffles so captivated Marina's senses that she uncontrollably asked, indeed demanded, that Mark immediately park their car and join the human parade to the nearest cafe-patio to enjoy a drink before they met their friends from Acerenza for a late evening Neapolitan dinner.

Easier said than done, however, Mark thought as he desperately looked in all directions for a few spare feet to park. He knew that finding a parking spot anywhere near Piazza Garibaldi on a Friday evening would be an impossible ordeal. He could see cars and scooters by the dozens haphazardly abandoned by their owners on sidewalks, in front of blatant and threatening signs forbidding parking, across residential and commercial driveways and wherever else there was even the slightest opening.

As a result, Mark instead drove past Naples' main railway station, *Stazione Centrale,* and continued several streets behind it where the area degenerated somewhat into semi-lit narrow lanes and vendors catering largely to locals.

With the dexterity and fearlessness of a true *Napoletano,* Mark guided the car to their hotel *Albergo Due Notti*, a clean and unpretentious hotel serving mainly Italian business people.

There, Mark parked his car safely in the underground garage and proceeded to check in both themselves and their friends Luca and Anna who would be arriving by train to join them shortly.

Luca had told Mark that he had spent several years as a teenager apprenticing as an office clerk in Naples with his uncle, before deciding that he could not bear to be away from his beloved Anna. He therefore cut short his apprenticeship, and possible government career, in favor of a less glamorous life in Acerenza, but one in union with the woman he adored.

But despite his absence from Naples for many years, Luca still remembered the best pizzeria; the best *pasticceria*; and, although a never-ending debate among Neapolitans, the spot that served absolutely the best espresso in Naples and therefore, at least according to Neapolitans, in the whole world.

Luca had invited Mark to spend time together in Naples and had planned for them a weekend to savor life "*alla Napoletana*".

There would be just enough time for Mark and Marina to walk over to a nearby cafe in the piazza where, over an *aperitivo*, they would await the arrival of their friends before heading out to dinner.

Luca had seen to it that weekend experiences were in store for the four friends, experiences that would depict for them the true character of this flamboyant and infinitely charismatic people.

CHAPTER 14

The train from Potenza to Naples had arrived almost thirty minutes late, explained Luca Moranni when he and Anna finally joined their friends at the neighborhood cafe, after they checked into their hotel.

Mark and Marina had hardly noticed their friends' late arrival, however. They had been preoccupied by the outdoor theatre that was Naples. Drink in hand, they witnessed the endless parade of activity before them—a seemingly chaotic and directionless flow of people, cars and motorcycles of every type and color and moving in every direction, as if on double time. Everyone, it appeared, was busy in a helter-skelter spectrum of activities that created energy but, seemingly, without any precise objective. A Vespa would pass by them at break-neck speed only to screech to an immediate stop to allow its driver and lady passenger to chat with friends they had seen, without any hurry and in total contradiction to the daredevil speed at which their two-wheeler had been manoeuvred moments earlier.

This was an energetic and hyperactive community acting in a type of caffeinated *dolce far niente*—hurrying to nowhere, busy at nothing.

There was a palpable, frenetic pace everywhere. A pace, though, that Mark felt did not lead to any ambitious objectives other than the wish, indeed the need, to live for the moment, to enjoy life at full speed and at its fullest, without worrying about what tomorrow might bring. Tomorrow would open a new chapter of experiences and activities for these proud and scurrying *Napoletani*. And thus, their recurring life cycle would continue, from one day to the next to the next, as it had in like manner, for many centuries.

"Very close to Piazza Garibaldi, I used to take Anna on special occasions when it was important to impress her . . .", Luca winked at his wife as he lovingly placed his hand over her shoulder. Luca had planned a festive dinner experience that would allow his friends to savor the taste and smells of a typical Neapolitan meal.

True Neapolitan cuisine has given birth to some of the most well-known dishes in the world. As perhaps Naples' most famous contribution to the world's culinary delights, *pizza alla Margherita* was originally created in honor of Margherita di Savoia, Italy's first queen. In its most authentic version, it is a simple concoction of dough with basil, mozzarella and tomatoes—green, white and red, representing the "*tricolore*", the colors of the Italian flag. But while the *Margherita* is the world's most well-known pizza, it is not the unanimous choice of carbo-loving Neapolitans. Margherita's main rival is the even simpler version, without mozzarella: a chewy dough, crusty and lightly burned around the exterior edges with basil and a light sprinkle of oregano with a drizzle of hot chillies-spiked pure virgin olive oil from neighboring Basilicata or Puglia.

The battle between these two worthy carbohydrate contestants has been known to cause friction even among friends and family—as each side proffers subtle nuances to the aromatic flavorings of one versus the other. These culinary battles have carried over to the "*pizzaioli*"—pizza-makers or masters, as they are often called—with many pizza-masters refusing to create the other version as being unworthy of their respective creative talents.

A short walk from the centre of Piazza Garibaldi, the four friends walked in unison, arm-in-arm as was the custom, toward Via Alfonso d'Aragona, where at Number 21 is one of Naples' landmark eateries: *Mimmi Alla Ferrovia*, their dinner destination.

As they entered the restaurant, Luca and Anna sprinted ahead and were greeted by the affable owner, Nunzio. Luca introduced his friends Marco and Marina as two Italians who had returned to their homeland after many successes in America . . . and the owners of Santiana-Vino, the very winery from which Luca had persuaded Nunzio to purchase some of the restaurant's wine inventory.

On hearing Luca's introduction, Nunzio hugged Mark and Marina as if they were long-lost blood relatives and proceeded to take the group to a private corner table where Nunzio proudly announced: "*Cari amici, stasera ci pensa Nunzio*"—"my dear friends, leave tonight's dinner selection to Nunzio".

Within minutes, a large steaming plate of "*spaghetti alla puttanesca*" was placed in the middle of the table. As the aroma of freshly-cooked olives and capers filled the lungs, Nunzio re-emerged from the kitchen to serve the pasta and, at the same time, to allocate to each a large slice of the local favorite "*pizza fritta*", fried pizza, to accompany the pasta appetizer.

By this time, the eatery was bustling with local patrons and the hive of activity produced an incessant combination of sound and movement that titillated the senses. Servers balancing steaming plates of fresh pasta with *antipasti* of Caprese salads made with local "*latte di bufala*"—buffalo milk, tomato and basil sprinkled with the purest virgin olive oil. The crescendo of sound reverberating in the room and Nunzio's warm embraces to most of the patrons created a festive and familial atmosphere, one of a private dinner party with selected guests eager to express their effusiveness, to please, to charm and to be charmed. In short, a place where people were in a hurry to do nothing except to enjoy the moment, to savor every expression of passion, to participate in every discussion within their immediate friends or family at their own table or within their new "extended families" at adjacent tables.

Magically, it seemed, Nunzio appeared with a bottle of *Lacrima Christi*—Christ's Tear—for his four special guests.

"Dear friends", he began, "this is Campania's best-known white wine. It's no ordinary wine, of course. It is a holy wine, a spiritual wine. It is named "*Lacrima Christi*" because Christ himself was so taken by the indescrible beauty of our Bay of Naples, his body now stiffening with pride, that he could not contain himself and began weeping over its beauty and over the many sins of the inhabitants of Naples . . .". With a mischievous smile on his lips and a glitter in his eyes, Nunzio repeated ". . . yes, my friends, Christ wept both because of the beauty of our City and over the poverty and misery of our people."

Mark had heard this refrain before and, while he demurred over its authenticity, he did notice that, in his recounting, Nunzio had replaced the words "sins" with "poverty and misery". Mark wondered whether Nunzio believed these were synonymous concepts in the minds of Neapolitans.

A large pot of steaming *Polipo In Guazzetto*—squid cooked in a light tomato sauce—arrived as the main event. The flavor and aroma of the herbs infused into the tomato sauce and the fresh squid created almost a sensual experience for the four friends. The wine Nunzio had chosen was a perfect accompaniment to a superb meal.

"Naples is famous for its *cucina povera*—poor man's food. It is simple and delicious because they use only locally-grown herbs and locally produced ingredients. "Nothing is imported outside a radius of a hundred miles", Anna reported mainly to Marina who had a deep interest in nutrition and everything organic. With this new information, Marina lifted her eyes upward and concluded simply "it is truly amazing how they can produce such a wonderful mixture of flavors with the simplest of ingredients. I can actually taste the purity of every item and yet they collectively form a combination that's impossible to duplicate in taste, smell and texture".

Over coffee and *sfogliatelle*—a local favorite of alternating thin layers of pastry and sweet cream—Luca began to update Mark on the financial and operational results of the grape harvest in Acerenza. Simply put, it had been an excellent year for both Santiana-Vino (the wine-producing and exporting business Mark had started in Acerenza) and for its affiliate, Santiana-Alimentari (the food exporting business). Luca explained: "We are penetrating even North America with our *Aglianico* brand. We are very competitive with our price point and we offer a moderately-priced quality option for the North American consumer". Mark marvelled at the progress his business lieutenant had made in his business acumen over the last few months.

Luca then reviewed the food exporting side of the business and offered his view that Santiana-Alimentari would soon become a major food exporting company that, more and more, would bring the Basilicata food specialties to the kitchens of people all over the world.

"When you come to Acerenza for the Christmas Holidays, we will provide full statements showing the numbers. You will be pleased, *caro Marco*. You have put Acerenza on the map. And soon we will have one of the largest food and wine companies in the *Mezzogiorno*—southern Italy—".

"And importantly, we have created over three hundred jobs for the Acerenzesi . . .", Mark concluded with a deep sense of satisfaction.

CHAPTER 15

As they lingered over coffee, Mark allowed present reality to take a breather and, for a short while, dug deep in his memory bank. He had become young Marco again. He imagined once again his trip with his grandfather half a century earlier when they had travelled to the nearby town of Pietragalla to hire men for the upcoming Vendemmia. Mark now recalled his grandfather's admonition: "Marco, never forget that when you deal with people, you have to be fair". Even as a very young boy, Mark had seen how his grandfather had quickly struck a bargain with the hired workers and offered them generous wages because it had been a good growing season that augured well for financial returns. It was natural, his grandfather had explained, to share their good fortune with the workers.

Mark—turned—Marco repeated in his mind his grandfather's notion of "fair bargain", the simple and unadulterated concept that one should act equitably, not because one is compelled to do so but because it is the right thing to do.

"*Volete qualcos' altro*?"—would you like anything else-, offered the effervescent server. Mark snapped shut his memory movie reel and, turning alternately to Marina and the Moranni's, said: "Let's do something really special. Luca, from what you have told me, we will have an excellent season for both companies. We should share our good fortune by opening a Santiana Store in Acerenza that carries all our products—wine, cheeses and all the other foods we produce. We should sell these foods and wine at subsidized prices that will be significantly less than even our own production costs, to make sure that all Acerenzesi can afford them . . .". Luca, the recently-honed business executive, sat up and looked intently at his friend: "Marco, this is an excellent idea, but how do we stop people from other towns from coming to Acerenza and buying from our store food and wine at the same lower prices we sell to our home town residents?"

Mark recalled his grandfather's other lessons: *treat others with dignity and with generosity. Share your bounty with others without expecting anything in return. Do so not out of compulsion but simply because it's the right thing to do.* Mark turned to his friend Luca, smiled and said softly: "We can't. And we shouldn't."

My grandfather would be pleased, Mark thought.

The four friends thanked their host Nunzio for the memorable evening and walked out in the crisp late autumn night, all the while chatting and making plans for their reunion in Acerenza for the Christmas festivities that would include the sharing of special spiritual bonding with their friends.

Christmas time was a special time of year in Acerenza and Mark and Marina intended to turn it into a permanent tradition as often as possible.

PART 2

CHAPTER 16

Half-way across the Atlantic Ocean, the *Alitalia* crew on the flight from Rome to Toronto had gathered at the rear of the aircraft trading individual stories and generally talking "shop".

The aircraft was scarcely half full, with a scattering of business executives and regular passengers using Rome as a convenient connecting point to Toronto from Asia and the Middle East.

Early March was generally not a favored time of year to be visiting this part of the world. Winter still had a tight grip on central Canada. It would still be three weeks before spring would perk up sufficient courage to make its seasonal debut, and several more weeks before it would confidently advance without the fear of intermittent retreats.

Mark and his wife, too tired to be active but too excited to sleep, passed the hours in that delicious semi-awareness and unconsciousness that allows one to hear voices around them that are collective rather than individual, and that form an indistinguishable amalgamation of surrounding sound, much like an orchestral background.

Mark and Marina were returning home to settle personal matters resulting from their trans-location to Southern Italy. They had embraced their decision to visit their daughter Dior and to spend some time with their friends and family with whom they had kept in contact during their absence.

It had been a year since Mark and Marina had returned to Italy where, in Tuscany, they had re-immersed themselves in the philosophy and culture of the Italian Renaissance, that mixture of art, music, philosophy, science and culture that had transformed the world and that had provided a revolution of awareness pulling the world from the comforts of the Dark Ages into a new era of fresh ideas, of scientific and artistic risk, of personal and collective growth the likes of which mankind had not theretofore witnessed.

For Mark and Marina, reliving these experiences through study and reflection had allowed them to again re-awaken a part of their lives that had been so important to them in their university years.

For Mark, this cultural renaissance had been a transforming personal experience. It had allowed him again to become the reflective undergraduate university student of yesteryear. It had turned Mark into the student of philosophy he had been more than four decades earlier, except now more mature and, therefore, more appreciative and more experienced, more able to apply the academic theories of philosophy into practice, using personal experiences as bases.

As a result, Mark had reluctantly decided to lay aside his innate ambitions that had propelled his past successes, in favor of a more balanced and spiritual existence.

It was in the mesmerizing splendor of the Tuscan hills that Mark had rediscovered Marco—that youthful idealism that, in the intervening busy decades had somehow escaped from his soul as he had marched toward the pinnacle of material and societal successes. As the years passed, his idealism had given way to a focused and relentless need to succeed. Spirituality had been vanquished by innate, raw ambition. The needs of the soul had been replaced by a feeding frenzy that had no objective other than to win.

"Would you like a hot snack before we land, Signori?", asked the amiable Italian flight attendant as she began her final round of service before readying for the landing in Toronto. "*Grazie, no*", replied Mark instinctively in Italian.

A year in Italy had transformed Mark's primary instincts into using his native tongue first. It would be a few days back in Canada before Mark would be able to adapt and reconvert his primary automatic instincts back to English. "A glass of sparkling water, *per piacere*", added Mark, consciously transitioning between the two languages, a transition that symbolized the hybrid nature of his very being.

The flight tracker on their personal screen showed they had reached Canadian land mass. They felt excited. They would soon be landing at home.

Mark tightened his grip on Marina's hand. She turned toward him and sensed a determined emotion flowing from her husband that told her he had returned to resolve important issues.

Marina instinctively felt that her husband would shortly be experiencing events that would likely complete his internal odyssey and that, perhaps, would finally and permanently put an end to his personal turbulence so as to allow him, at last, to find that seemingly fleeting peace of mind.

CHAPTER 17

"Where to, sir?" asked the taxi driver at the exit from Terminal 3 at Toronto Pearson International Airport.

Mark and Marina quickly settled in the back seat of the cab and shut the door to the raging blizzard outside. "Minus 18 with the wind chill . . . more snow all weekend", offered the driver matter-of-factly. "If we had good weather here in the winter, this would be the most populated country in the world", continued the monologue.

Talking about the weather has always been important to Canadians, Mark thought. Perhaps, its harshness and the inability to control it were the reasons why this otherwise mellow people continually showed passion for the topic.

"So much for global warming! Where is Mr. Gore in the winter months? He goes on vacation in the Caribbean for some warmth, I bet . . .", the driver continued with appropriate gesticulations, satisfied that he had conveyed to his captive passengers not only that he was a closet meteorologist but also an expert in global warming.

As the taxi inched its way along the busy highway that had been hampered by rush-hour traffic and aggravated by the snow, Mark's memories flooded back. Familiar places, the large mall to the right where Marina and Mark had shopped for many years came into view; the nearby hotel where they had celebrated their wedding so many years ago; the southbound expressway that Marina had led an unsuccessful petition to stop its construction during those rebellious student days. A turn in the road; a speeding ticket once given by a grim police officer; a corner cafe that no longer was. These seemingly commonplace items that bore no importance when Mark lived in Canada now achieved in his mind focus and attention. "I am just realizing how homesick I've been, Mark", Marina said softly and almost apologetically. "I love Italy but I miss my country, I miss my home and I miss the life we had built here". As Marina spoke haltingly, she intently stared out the car window as if she were seeing for the first time points she had routinely seen, without much attention, a thousand times before. "Me too", replied Mark.

Within a few minutes, they were opening the door to their home; that fortress of memories that had earlier shaped their life as a family.

As they entered the house, they both knew that there was now no turning back to Mark's completion of his unfinished business.

CHAPTER 18

Although at a distance, Mark had been closely following his daughter's career path. Dior had become a bright and energetic young woman, with her mother's kindness and generosity and with Mark's burning ambition to succeed. Even as a fifteen year-old, Dior had shown an acumen and fearlessness for decision-making that reminded Mark of his own youth. Mark had never been afraid to venture into new paths rather than following traditional ones. He had always been excited by newness, in whatever form: the thinking of ideas outside the box and expressing them more creatively than others; or the formulating of innovative concepts that branded him either as a reflective and fearless warrior or as an overly ambitious and reckless fool.

Dior was thriving at Merkson LLC, the reputable consulting company that Santius had retained to investigate and formulate the company's new strategic direction a year earlier. The very strategy that had been the catalyst to Mark's resignation and to his ensuing spiritual journey.

Over the course of the past year, Dior had shown herself to be tenacious in her positions but, at the same time, reflective and mature in the way she advanced her ideas. Nevertheless, in spite of her aggressiveness, Dior had demonstrated to her colleagues, to her clients and to her superiors that she would never cross that invisible, yet well-defined, line separating ethical conduct from immoral behavior. Dior was ambitious and fearless but she never allowed herself to believe that the end justified the means. For her, reaching a corporate objective was all important, but not if the process to attain that objective was contaminated in any way.

Moreover, Dior never believed that otherwise unacceptable actions could somehow become justified by lending a "blind eye" to such activities.

"Dad", Dior explained to her father over breakfast the morning following his return to Toronto, "there is such tremendous pressure put on us by clients and by the firm to fulfil the clients' wishes at any cost". Dior paused for a second and then continued: "Clients retain us to investigate issues objectively, but then expect certain conclusions that they had already reached privately". She toyed with her slice of toast and then looked straight into her father's eyes burning them with her own laser beams. "Certain clients are ready to pay hundreds of thousands of dollars to have us undertake countless hours of supposed-objective research, only to later use their expensive retainers as a subtle but persuasive influence to have our firm sign off on a conclusion that they had reached even before hiring us. Essentially, they are glad to pay multiple six figures to get research recommendations that they can then trumpet to their own boards of directors, or to their shareholders, as so-called objective conclusions derived by a reputable consulting firm. They are buying our letterhead more than the substance of the report".

Mark listened thoughtfully, cupped his chin, placed his hand over his daughter's and replied: "Dior, it's a difficult lesson in life that you're experiencing. Always remember, though, as you sort out these issues on your own that the otherwise thoughtful Italian philosopher, Nicolo'

Macchiavelli, had it all wrong. The end doesn't always justify the means. Your personal reputation is built on integrity. Material wealth may seem essential at the time but its importance quickly fades because it doesn't, by itself, fulfil the needs of the soul. Only personal satisfaction and spiritual fulfillment have that magical power . . .".

As Mark spoke, his eyes glazed over. Dior knew that her father had been transported back by deep thought into the voyages he had recently been experiencing during his internal journey.

She let him continue in his reflection for a while, undisturbed, and then whispered: "I've missed you so much, Daddy", as she tightened her grip on her father's hands.

CHAPTER 19

"*Buon Giorno, Mark, come stai? Quando sei ritornato dall'Italia?*"—How are you Mark, when did you return from Italy?—asked the affable Fabrizio as he hugged his old friend.

"I returned a few days ago with Marina. We're back for a short time to visit our daughter Dior and to settle some personal affairs", replied Mark.

Fabrizio's Ristorante had been a favorite lunch spot for Mark during his tenure as CEO of Santius; a second office where Mark had conducted negotiations over major and lesser corporate deals. It had not been uncommon for Mark to ink multi-million dollar transactions literally on the back of a napkin, all the while nibbling on a *caprese* salad and cheese *focaccia* and sipping on his usual glass of *San Pellegrino.*

Indeed, Mark had been such a frequent patron at Fabrizio's that its owner always kept reserved a corner table for Mark—known internally as the Santius satellite office—with a permanent "reserved" sign prominently displayed on the crisp Italian linen tablecloth.

"Your usual table is ready", Fabrizio announced proudly as he led his long-time patron and friend toward the back of the restaurant. "I hope you won't be ordering *pappardelle al cinghiale*—pappardelle pasta with wild boar ragu sauce—for your guest today, chuckled Fabrizio with a wink.

The last time Mark had dined at Fabrizio's was when he had that fateful meeting with Burton Cavendish, chairman of Santius' board of directors, a year earlier. Fabrizio's reference to the *pappardelle al cinghiale* was Fabrizio's loose translation of "pappardelle with pig sauce", intended to indicate Fabrizio's personal expression of disgust toward Cavendish's boorish behavior that day.

CHAPTER 20

As he waited for his lunch companion, Mark reflected back on the life-changing events he had experienced during the last many months. Mark felt comfortable with his decision never to compromise his ethics in favor of person material gain. Mark had come to believe that there are issues of personal morality and integrity that transcend one's drive to profit; that ambition requires to be controlled to ensure that it does not become Machiavellian in believing that reaching an objective is the only thing that counts, no matter how it is achieved.

Fabrizio interrupted Mark's reflections by appearing with a glass of Santiana's own Aglianico and bottle of *San Pellegrino.* As he filled Mark's glass with water, he said "Mr. Ruprech called to send his apologies, Mark. He'll be a few minutes late".

CHAPTER 21

A year earlier, after a thorough search for candidates to replace Mark as CEO, the Santius Board settled on Tony Ruprech, who had been serving as the company's Chief Operating Officer during Mark's tenure, to succeed him in that position. The only dissenting vote came, expectedly, from Burton Cavendish who passionately argued that it would best for Santius to bring in a fresh face—unaffiliated by friendship or history with Mark Gentile—to ensure that Santius stayed the old course. After all, Santius had travelled on a lengthy and uninterrupted path of profitability over many years, Cavendish had argued, so why detour it in a different direction as Mark Gentile had recommended? And why appoint Tony Ruprech as CEO when he had been so closely associated with Mark's late-blooming strategy of altering the proven direction of the company and thereby driving it into financial chaos?

Nevertheless, and in spite of Cavendish's self-serving oratorical skills, the rest of his Board had remained unconvinced. While the remaining members of Cavendish's Board had reluctantly supported their chairman in rejecting Mark Gentile's wish to quickly engage in a dramatic change in corporate direction, nevertheless, over the longer term, they had little doubt that Mark Gentile's decision to have Santius find a new niche within which to produce automobiles had merit and deserved further consideration. Tony at the helm of Santius would ensure continuing monitoring of the issue, they secretly felt.

Still, Cavendish had continued with his impassioned plea: "After all, dear colleagues," Cavendish had submitted, "wasn't Tony Ruprech as responsible as Mark Gentile in attempting to take our company into a path of debt for the business and a substantially lower share price for our shareholders? How do we know that Ruprech won't take us on exactly the same disastrous financial path that his boss, Mark Gentile, had devised and that he had himself supported?"

Nevertheless, and in spite of Cavendish's plea to find an external replacement as the new CEO, the rest of the Board decided that Tony Ruprech, a loyal and competent senior executive of Santius for many years, deserved the opportunity to lead the company in what were likely to be turbulent times ahead. A leader, they argued, who had experience and who commanded internal respect from management were deemed to be the overriding criteria. And in this topsy-turvy nomination and selection process that pitted Cavendish against the rest of his Board, Tony Ruprech was elected the new CEO of Santius.

In fact, while not overtly expressed by any of the Board members, a number of them had favored Mark's strategic plan, perhaps with minor modifications as to the timing of its implementation. They were caught off guard when Mark made his decision to resign so abruptly without any forewarning and without offering any resistance.

Their chairman had never reported to the rest of the Board the discussion that he had had with Mark at Fabrizio's. Cavendish had not disclosed to them his request that Mark immediately announce his intention to renounce the implementation of his declared new strategy. Cavendish had never explained to the Board the genesis of Mark's resignation letter, nor that Cavendish had orchestrated the scheme by which Mark had been left no option but to resign.

As for Mark, at the time he gave his written resignation, he had no way of knowing that the committee of independent directors had never met, contrary to what Cavendish had told him. Cavendish had used this manoeuvre to clothe himself with the supposed Board authority in order to extract Mark's direct revocation of his intention to take Santius in a new direction or, alternatively if he refused to do so, to subtly but nonetheless aggressively, force Mark's resignation. At the time, Mark had no idea that Cavendish had unilaterally and secretly concocted this scheme and that he was implementing it totally without the Board's knowledge. In fact, the rest of the Board had no idea at the time, nor were they told subsequently, that Cavendish had taken it upon himself to meet with Mark at Fabrizio's that fateful day in order to force Mark's retraction of his public statement to the shareholders.

Mark had suspected, but had no basis for asserting publicly, that Cavendish was afraid that Mark, if he were allowed to continue to lead Santius, would likely interfere with Cavendish's personal plans to seek personal enrichment from his substantial equity portfolio.

The reality was that Cavendish had been terrified at the prospect of a falling stock price and from the uncertainty as to how long it would take for Mark's strategic plan to gain traction and thereby cause a rebound in the stock price and, therefore, on his personal wealth. Simply put, Cavendish's personal time horizon did not coincide with Mark's timetable to implement his vision for a new corporate direction. Mark's plan was a long-term strategy intended to benefit all shareholders of the company. On the other hand, Cavendish's personal plan involved an extremely tight schedule strictly intended to allow him to cash out at the earliest opportunity.

Cavendish had decided that, at his advanced age, he could not wait for long-term corporate strategies to take hold. He couldn't afford to take the risks that were implicit in Mark's strategy. To eliminate these risks, Cavendish had concluded that he needed to remove Mark Gentile from his leadership position or, better still, to cause Mark to remove himself, so as to avoid controversy within the company's Board and Management.

CHAPTER 22

Mark's strongly-held view that Santius would not be able to survive unless it immediately switched into producing alternate-energy vehicles had become a reality much quicker than even Mark had imagined.

Following Mark's departure from the company, at several automobile and technology conferences in both the United States and Europe, the focus of the biggest car makers had been the introduction of prototype models powered by electricity, biofuels and hybrids combining non-fossil energy with gasoline. Certain events in the last year since Mark's departure from Santius had reaffirmed Mark's original analysis. Political disruptions in Iran caused by massive citizens protests had wreaked political and social havoc in that oil rich country, as well as overall instability throughout the Middle East.

Moreover, revolts against the rulers in Syria, Libya, Egypt, some of the Emirates and northern Africa had created a powder keg that had resulted in turbulence and volatility with the supply of oil throughout the world. Massive consumers like China and India began blatant campaigns to increase their oil inventory, thereby driving up even more dramatically the price of oil. As a result, it was not unusual for gasoline prices at the pump to fluctuate by up to a dollar a gallon from week to week. As the geopolitical situation became more or less inflamed by the unpredictable circumstances of the day, the price at the pumps became more and more a roller coaster of volatility.

And so, the push for more energy-efficient automobiles became an obsession for consumers, and therefore, for auto manufacturers. Politicians, partly to gain favor with voters, often threatened that the United States would never become captive to Middle East extortion. Directly and indirectly, various United States government officials routinely began to indicate publicly the absolute need for an integrated American strategy on alternate fuel and energy self-sufficiency for the United States.

Car companies that had once focused on larger vehicles without regard to either the environment or the price of fuel, were now downsizing their products and trumpeting the need for lighter and more efficient methods of transportation. Even public transport buses and government automobiles were either being converted to hybrid energy engines or totally to electricity.

This cycle became a self-fulfilling prophecy. The more instability the world created, the more unpredictability resulted in the automobile industry. The American consumers' mindset was rapidly changing. It would not be very long, energy gurus predicted, before alternate energy vehicles would predominate the North American, and therefore the world, automobile market.

Moreover, these volatile and often turbulent global circumstances had passionate voices that aided and abetted them: conservationists and even strident eco-maniacs, now had the podium with newly-acquired credibility in advocating their prediction that, within ten years, not a drop of oil would be used to drive American cars.

Mark's bold prediction that a dramatically new path was needed for Santius in order that it could survive in a rapidly-changing world was quickly becoming a reality. In fact, this reality had occurred much more quickly than even Mark had predicted.

Mark's fear that Santius must immediately adopt an alternate energy strategy so as to remain relevant had sent shockwaves among the company's investors when he announced it a year earlier because of the uncertainty that it created. Mark knew that his new strategy would, at first, be hard to embrace because people normally found comfort in the certainty of the status quo. Nevertheless, Mark knew all too well that if there were to be further delays in implementing the switch away from fossil fuel, Santius would be squeezed out of business by its bigger and more resilient competitors.

CHAPTER 23

The scenario at Fabrizio's a year earlier had been devised by Cavendish and played out by him alone from start to finish.

On that occasion, Cavendish had prepared himself well for his critical meeting with Mark. In his due diligence on Mark, Cavendish had discovered that even a remote puncturing of Mark's sense of ethics and morality would be sufficient to trigger an internal deliberation on his part that would ultimately lead to his resignation. Cavendish had justified his actions by reasoning that, after all, as chairman of Santius' board of directors, he had the right to assume authority to accomplish an objective that, he reasoned, was clearly for the best interests of the company and its shareholders. After all, did he not have the mandate, indeed the legal obligation, to protect at all costs the financial interests of all the shareholders, including himself? While his personal interests would be greatly advanced by maintaining the *status quo* with Santius's old strategic direction, he believed that the best interests of all shareholders squared exactly with his own objectives. Cavendish had persuaded himself that preserving the company's stock price and future earnings trajectory could be maintained only if no dramatic changes were made to the company's corporate direction.

In the end, Cavendish had concluded that Mark would be a substantial obstacle to his personal, short-term plan and that he must therefore be sacrificed for the greater good of all shareholders, including himself. The best way to accomplish this, Cavendish had reasoned, was to force a course of action that he knew would ultimately cause Mark a personal moral crisis. Cavendish had been certain that he could drive Mark into a self-analysis that would result in his voluntarily severing his tenure with Santius. Mark's departure would put an end to the proposed new strategy that Mark had concocted. In turn, this would allow Cavendish to stay the course and, thereby, to keep Santius's current stock price afloat. As a direct consequence, his personal net worth would be preserved and, perhaps, quickly increased.

Cavendish's plan had worked to perfection. By requesting that Mark publicly renege for good on his new strategic plan for Santius that he had announced to its shareholders, Cavendish knew that Mark's personal ethics would get in the way of now rejecting the very strategic change he had recommended. This, Cavendish had suspected, Mark would never allow himself to do. The result was, expectedly, immediate. Mark's resignation, without rancor and without vindictiveness, paved the way for Cavendish to confirm his full control over the direction of the company.

Importantly, Cavendish's devious plan would ensure that Santius' share price would not be negatively impacted in the short term so as to allow Cavendish to cash out his considerable stock portfolio before he could safely resign as chairman of the board and, thereafter, enjoy the fruits of his labor in his retirement.

Cavendish would soon learn, however, that even the most carefully constructed plans can go awry, and that there is often no financial reward when financial goals are achieved through unsavory schemes devoid of morality and ethics.

CHAPTER 24

As Mark sat at his table at Fabrizio's waiting for Tony to arrive, he fiddled with his newest toy, his omnipresent Playbook tablet. Mark had quickly learned the advantages of a mobile personal device and had downloaded all his Santiana files so that he could review the status of his Italian companies at any time, anywhere in the world. In this way, he could operate his Santiana businesses continually, keep in touch with friends and family and keep current with news from the four corners of the globe.

As Mark became engrossed in replying to Santiana-Alimentari's marketing director in Acerenza on a promotional initiative being undertaken for its products, Tony Ruprech, beaming from ear to ear, arrived and extended both arms to embrace his friend: "Welcome back, Mark. We have all missed you. I am so happy to see you." And then with his usual critical eye, he continued: "Mark, you look great. You've lost a few pounds and you look lean and hungry".

Mark was delighted to see his old friend again. While they had exchanged emails in the past few months, both had been busy: Tony in attempting to keep the Santius ship from sinking; Mark in finding a safe harbor from navigating in his own sea of internal turbulence. The first, trying to fill the company's coffers with material wealth; the other, trying to fill the spiritual void in his soul.

The two friends caught up on each other's personal lives without a word about Santius. Nevertheless, they both knew that Santius would eventually dominate their attention.

"How are you enjoying your new life, Mark?" Tony asked, not so much to make conversation but because he was genuinely interested in his friend's activities over the past year. Tony became captivated by Mark's recounting of the life he had been experiencing in his native land during the past year.

Tony and Mark ventured into a discussion of corporate-related issues. Tony vividly described the events following Santius's shareholders' meeting a year earlier, including Cavendish's manoeuvres to be rid of Mark in order to safely fulfil his personal greed without opposition.

"The global events of the last year have proved you right, Mark. You predicted that turbulence in the world would create a volatility that, in turn, would drive up the price of fossil fuel and, with it, the price at the pumps," Tony said emphatically. "The Middle East and Africa are now the new boiling cauldron", continued Mark "fear and greed predominate over logic and common sense. China and other developing countries continue to stockpile oil for fear that their economic development will be stalled. Oil producing nations, particularly the more aggressive rebels among them, are taking advantage of this perceived fear and are spreading even more fear and greed by cutting back on oil production". Tony added his own perspective: "It's a never-ending cycle that builds on itself. The result is that gasoline is now retailing at new highs and there doesn't seem to be an end in sight".

Whimsically, Mark replied: "This is precisely why I wanted Santius to enter the world of alternate energy. This is the reason why I wanted to convert our car engines from fossil fuel to alternative energy sources such as electric and biofuels; why it was essential for the company to form a partnership with these types of alternate energy developers so as to remain at the forefront of this type of new technology."

As Mark spoke, Tony could see a dramatic transformation in Mark's demeanor. His passion, his personal energy and his tenacity, all visible characteristics of old Mark, were again resurfacing and becoming etched on Mark's brow.

In a staccato style of delivery, employed by Mark whenever he needed to make an emphatic comment, Mark began: "Sure, this new direction for Santius would have meant short-term sacrifice for the company and its shareholders. Substantial capital expenditures would have indeed cut deeply into Santius' profitability and, therefore, would likely have temporarily shaved off substantial value off its share price. But this was necessary medicine that could mean the difference between corporate wellness and death", Mark concluded, as he stared deeply into Tony's eyes.

On hearing these words, Tony felt optimistic that Mark's determination might well indicate that he could be ready to postpone his continued recusal from corporate life and assume the gargantuan challenge Tony had come to discuss.

"*Amici*—friends", Fabrizio reluctantly said as he approached the table, "all this talk and no food is not good for your health, and is not so good for Fabrizio's pocketbook either". And with a mischievous smile, Fabrizio announced to his special guests that he had personally taken care of choosing lunch for them. On cue, a waiter appeared with two appetizer plates of grilled calamari on a bed of arugula salad. No sauces, no dressings—pure food with only slices of lemon and drizzled pure virgin olive oil to enhance the taste.

"*Buon appetito,*" pronounced Fabrizio solemnly as the bitter arugula intermingled with the warm calamari created a cloud of aroma that wafted throughout the restaaurant.

CHAPTER 25

Over lunch, the two long-standing friends and business colleagues continued to recount important incidents in their respective lives over the past year.

Tony marvelled, but was not shocked, to hear that Mark had put in place a full infrastructure in Acerenza to start his Santiana businesses—first Santiano-Vino, the wine-making and wine exporting company and shortly thereafter, Santiana-Alimentari, the food production and export business. Both businesses, Mark had explained, were now bringing the Basilicata wines, foods and spices to every corner of Europe, North America and, in short order, to most regions in the world.

"How did you manage getting so much accomplished so quickly"—enquired Tony. "Wasn't one of the more important reasons why you left Santius to return to Italy to find a balance between work and play?" continued Tony with an enquiring smile. The questions were direct and were intended to draw from Mark a response that would tell Tony whether his friend was ready to resume the corporate life he had left behind, the life Mark had so treasured for such a long period in his life.

Before discussing the current issues Santius was facing, Tony needed to understand Mark's future plans before he could disclose his own plans for Santius and the important role that Mark could play in helping him implementing them.

Mark reflected on Tony's questions and then slowly explained: "Tony, the main reason I left Santius when I did was because I felt my ethics were being compromised by Burton". Mark unconsciously used the familial first name reference to his old corporate adversary, Burton Cavendish. Mark stopped for a moment, ordered a round of espresso coffees. He then continued: "Burton manipulated me and used my tenure in Santius to achieve his purely personal objective of accumulating wealth for himself at all costs. And, at first, I let him do it. I knew what he was doing and why he was doing it and yet I allowed him continue toward his selfish objectives. I should have stopped him cold. Fortunately, personal ethics and morality eventually rang so loudly in my soul that they wouldn't let me have peace of mind without forcing me to reconsider my own behavior". Mark was now back to those gut-wrenching days following the Santius' shareholders meeting, pensive and with a look of distance in his eyes.

"I snapped out of it, Tony. I had been in a trance—in a state between consciousness and dream. In the end, to preserve my own personal dignity, I had only one option: leave Santius as quickly as possible so as to avoid the disastrous result of pitting management against its board of directors." As Mark completed this last statement, Tony could see that his friend was reliving the relief he had felt on that fateful day when he had submitted his letter of resignation.

The espresso coffees arrived and Mark noticed that Fabrizio had "performed" them perfectly "*corti*"—short—thick and foamy, just like he had been accustomed to enjoying them in his native land. In Italy, Mark had come to realize, a *barista* held a position of privilege. He didn't just make coffee. He performed an essential rite; he undertook a respected activity that resulted in either supreme satisfaction or utter contempt on the part of the customer. It was for this reason, that many Italians would travel from one end of town to the other in order to enjoy their favorite brew, a concoction that was usually ingested with one or two swirls of the cup and then in one swift and uninterrupted gulp. Fabrizio, it seemed, had mastered the same art and had graduated "*summa cum laude*", with the highest honors, from the school of espresso creation.

Mark stirred the espresso with a swift rotation of the cup and then downed the black liquid gold in one motion. Seemingly re-energized by the caffeine, Mark continued: "And in those days, it never occurred to me that I should try to find a balance between work and play—Tony", Mark offered with a slight smile. He then explained: "I realized that my experience with Cavendish had left a void in my inner being. I realized that my past ambitions had all merged to achieve societal success and material wealth. I began to feel that this void in my soul needed to be filled through a more balanced and introspective lifestyle. I looked in the mirror and I didn't like what I saw. I needed a drastic change in my life".

Tony saw that Mark's far-away look had again enveloped his friend. "I decided that I had to find a new balance in my life that would allow me to temper ambition with spiritual and ethical values that had been lacking in my previous existence. I wanted desperately to regain the idealism I had once experienced as a young lad in my hometown of Acerenza—that youthful idealism that sought satisfaction through internal rewards and not simply from external goals. And I felt that the best environment for me to recreate that balance was most likely the place where I had originally experienced the activities that, as a young boy, had filled me with wondrous memories that remain vivid and intact to this day".

As Mark completed the recounting of his internal odyssey in his native land, it had become clear to Tony that Mark's internal turbulence had somewhat abated but had not been totally eradicated. Tony suspected that there was still an important part of Mark's journey that he needed to travel before his inner demons could be finally exorcized.

Tony felt confident that he had drawn up the perfect antidote for Mark's continuing malaise, and he intended to administer it in short order. But that would be left for another day. Tony felt that Mark still needed more time to regroup. Moreover, Tony concluded instinctively that he also needed time to determine how best to present to Mark the Santius agenda that he wished him to consider.

"Mark, I really enjoyed seeing you again. Thank you for lunch. Let's meet in a couple of days. I have a very important, and I believe interesting, proposition to make to you. First, though, I must finalize some details before discussing it with you".

The two friends thanked Fabrizio for his usual hospitality and agreed to meet again later in the week to continue their discussion.

As Mark climbed into his car for his drive home, he had the sensation that his life was again about to take an unexpected turn that could well allow him to reach that seemingly unattainable inner fulfilment. He felt as if an opportunity might be presented to him that would give him a second chance to define his true character as a person.

The subtle sound of a distant whisper was calling him back to take up imaginary arms against an invisible, but active, opponent that had taken up permanent residency, and lay indivisibly, in his soul.

PART 3

CHAPTER 26

From the window of his study on the second floor of his home, Mark was witnessing a blizzard raging outside. Five inches of snow, the weather forecast had said, with a wind chill for good measure.

It was late March in Toronto. The calendar indicated that the spring equinox had arrived. Mother Nature, however, had other ideas. It would be several weeks of additional flirting with the emotions of these hardy northerners before man and nature could safely feel secure that the corner had been finally turned for another year.

Winter, the season that best reflected the tenacity and strength of character of Canadians, was always quick to arrive and late to leave. Toward the end of its seasonal grip, winter unfailingly toyed with its victims' emotions, and then dashed their premature optimism. This favorite of seasons for Canadians would once again overstay its welcome, much like an initially-welcomed guest who decides that the party is so much fun that it should last a little, or even a lot, longer. A guest who continues to be in full swing, long after the last of the other guests had left.

Southern Italians, however, have no such affinity for winter's unpredictable vagaries. They have no patience for this unwelcome visitor who refuses to leave when his time was done. They reluctantly allow its entry in the first place, and quickly compel its departure at the earliest opportunity. Its seasonal sojourn is therefore invariably brief. Winter has long since learned that these otherwise generous inhabitants become largely inhospitable hosts soon after its initial visit and that it must therefore find residency elsewhere in the more northern latitudes, like Canada, where its arrival would be welcomed and its late departure tolerated.

CHAPTER 27

Below his window, Mark watched with fascination as a solitary figure, with his dog in tow, tightened his coat collar as he hurried his pace toward shelter.

The transparent veil of gently cascading flakes had now gathered more force, its transparency replaced by an opaqueness that intended to hide winter's seeming embarrassment for its late visit.

Mark, however, saw an irresistible purity in the scene below. He put on his winter armament and stepped outside to immerse himself in the splendor of the season. He walked slowly, savoring that delicious tingle on his cheeks; the melting of snow on his forehead; the exhaled vapor from his quickened breathing.

The street was desolate. Not a soul to be seen anywhere. Only the mellow lighting from partially obstructed streetlamps and the warm flickers from television sets in the homes provided any evidence that there was humanity inhabiting the area.

Thousands of miles away, though, the mountainsides of the Lucanian Apennines were resplendent with color and vibrancy. Fields of white flowers and flowering fruit trees of every imaginable hue were already cascading downward from the outskirts of Acerenza to the Bradano Valley far below.

The peacefulness of the painting, however, belied the frenetic pace of Acerenza's citizenry. Everyone, man and beast, had woken from their brief seasonal hibernation. Fields were being ploughed, seeds planted, vines sprayed, trees and vines pruned. This was, indeed, the area's busiest season when all their work, with nature's assistance, would be later converted into nature's reward.

Acerenza's cafes and barber shops, traditional hives of gossip in January and February, were once again centres of need, not leisure. The Acerenzesi were now a busy lot; a quick greeting among one another would have to suffice for now, as they hurried through the narrow cobblestone streets toward their respective destinations. There would be plenty of time in the evening as they all assembled for the nightly *passeggiata* for them to ask about one another's health, and generally to catch up on current local gossip.

CHAPTER 28

Luca Moranni was a busy man these days. Santiana-Vino and Santiana-Alimentari were both rapidly growing enterprises. The two companies were separate entities but were both administered under a common organization. Luca Moranni was the designated corporate general for both. He ruled these consolidated businesses with a firmness and talent that belied his lack both of experience in the world of business and of educational schooling. For Luca, there had been none of the mandatory MBA programs; no business internships; no experience-gathering through the hierarchical corporate ladder. Instead, Luca used his practical logic, his amiability with people and his unfailing sense of what was right as the tools he employed to move the businesses forward.

As well, Luca had often heard from Mark stories of his grandfather's lessons and of the resulting instincts, inculcated into Mark at an early age, to detect right from wrong. Luca had witnessed how Mark had often obsessed on life's needing a sense of ethics, a sense of propriety in order for it to be truly fulfilling. Luca had seen how Mark's actions were always guided by his unquestioned acceptance of principled morality. Whenever possible, Luca had sought to emulate these same virtues in his own business dealings.

Luca Moranni, it seemed, had accepted Mark's notion that Nicolo' Machiavelli's edicts in his work, The Prince, that "*the end always justifies the means*" should have no substantive role to play in one's life; that business success could well be achieved in the context of ethics and morality; and that external rewards gained at the expense of these essential spiritual virtues, in the end, would never be able to truly fulfil one's spiritual needs.

In Luca, Mark had found a willing student who readily accepted Mark's lessons and those of Mark's grandfather and who, in turn, employed them in his business activities discharged both on behalf of Santiana and in living out his own life.

CHAPTER 29

"*Civil unrest in Iran threatens to overthrow the government regime . . . protestors in Libya and Syria have clashed with the government's armed forces . . . Egypt's President is in hiding as violence spreads throughout the country . . .*" blared Mark's television screen in his family room as he sat with his coffee early one morning.

Instant texting had become the new weapon replacing these now-seemingly obsolete war armaments. Word of small triumphs, or supplications for assistance could now travel to the four corners of the world through *Twitter* and other social media avenues faster than the wind. Instantaneous knowledge fed from blink-of-an-eye, externally-bound communication could now shape world events and geopolitical strategies. Supporters and detractors on all sides of a conflict could react instantly to news received on their mobile devices. On-line *chatters* and *twitters* wasted no time in recounting stories and experiences, often as they were occurring in real time and quite often exaggerated or understated, slanted one way or the other by purely personal leanings or beliefs.

The world had rapidly changed. There was now no time to wallow in reflection or demur on indolence. Delay could be fatal. One needed to keep up in order to be relevant, whether socially or in business. The world of instant communication, in turn, had now led to a world of instant information that, in turn, had resulted in a global society seeking immediate gratification. Delaying for hours, or even minutes, in taking action on important news now meant the difference between success and failure. Shades of grey; past gradations from success to failure and vice versa had disappeared. A "soft landing" was no longer possible, or acceptable. Triumph or destruction, polar extremes just a year or two earlier, now were the immediate result of receiving or not receiving instant dissemination of information and acting or not acting on such knowledge.

New armies waving hand-held technological devices were the new world conquerors. Brandishing traditional weapons was now left to professional fighters. The real power now lay in the hands of those who possessed knowledge and instant information with the ability to disseminate it effectively in real time all around the globe. Entire societies would be influenced and, indeed shaped, by pieces of hardware no bigger than the size of a cigarette package.

These were precisely the types of issues that had begun to alarm Mark a couple of years earlier, the very concerns that had motivated him to rethink Santius' future strategy. Mark had become convinced that potential disharmony in the Middle East and other hot spots would inevitably lead to societal turmoil and volatility that would impact the supply, and therefore the pricing, of oil. In turn, the supply of fossil-derived energy would become unpredictable because it would be dictated not by commerce's natural forces of supply and demand, but by the external geo-political influences of the day. These self-serving motivations would invariably lead to unmanageable volatility that would ultimately cause scarcity, followed by dramatic escalations in the price at the pump. As a result, national oil reserves would become depleted and, in a bid to replenish them, countries would drive up prices even further. The cycle would be self-feeding. And to fan these flames of rebellion among the desperate consumers and, further, to ensure that the flames would spread to engulf entire societies would be these small personal gadgets in the hands of reckless and unscrupulous mal-vivants who, with the flick of a key the size of a chickpea, had the power to change the world. This turn of events had been unimaginable just a few short years earlier.

And to further complicate the energy environment, countries such as India and China, as emerging and developing giants on the verge of fully industrializing almost one-half of the world's population, would continue to have an increasing metabolism that would see them devour all types of energy, particularly energy derived from fossil fuel, at an ever-accelerating pace. These factors, collectively, Mark had believed, would forever change the world's energy landscape. While governments had, for some time, paid lip-service to funding research for the development of alternative energy sources, Mark had concluded that, in the current world environment, the time had come for private enterprise to take action and become the driver of change. If politicians needed more confirmation of this newly-found attitude toward developing different energy sources, they needed only to look at their own national political landscapes where "Green Parties" were springing up as new political forces with which they were increasingly forced to deal.

It was also time for climate change, and the role that carbon emissions played within it, now needed to form important reference points in every politician's political agenda. Mark believed this was no longer an issue that could be avoided, or even postponed. Doing one's part to preclude further contamination of our world was no longer the domain of students and eccentrics. The issue had become mainstream and therefore needed to be confronted. Those who adopted quickly, Mark had concluded, would survive and flourish. Those who chose to remain loyal to the "old ways" would be left behind to wither and become irrelevant.

Faced with these concerns, Mark had feared for Santius' continued viability unless it immediately and dramatically altered its business strategy. Santius had been founded, and had thrived, on the concept of making small cars that were more fuel efficient than most of its competitors. For many years, as the car industry continued to fill North Americans' fascination with chrome and fins, Santius found its profitable niche by manufacturing smaller and lighter vehicles. However, with gas prices becoming more and more volatile and ultimately destined to increase dramatically, Mark felt that soon all the large auto makers would have little choice but to downsize and quickly squeeze out Santius from its niche market. The market would demand that this happen. It was an inevitability, Mark has reasoned.

Precisely in order to keep its competitive edge, Mark felt that it was time for Santius to adapt to this emerging reality, to become an industry leader once again by engaging entities that were on the leading edge of developing alternative energy sources of all types, biofuels and electric alike, and to jointly develop the next-generation car engine. Mark had clearly visualized the car of the future as having a new type of engine using non-traditional forms of energy sources such as ethanol, bio-butanol and electric. Early on, Mark had foreseen the development of hybrid engines that would be powered by a combination of traditional gasoline and one or more of these other sources.

Mark had reasoned that Santius must turn to this new strategy immediately so as to preserve its relevance and, therefore, its financial viability. The short-term financial pain it would inevitably suffer was necessary medicine needed to ensure its survival. Events in the past year since Burton Cavendish had manipulated his Board of Directors and Santius' shareholders in voting to preserve the company's status quo for fear of stock depreciation, had confirmed the views Mark had presented to the Board.

The price of oil had risen to an all-time high in the past few months, both on the commodities markets and, where it counted most, at the pump. It seemed to be an accepted reality that aggravated political instability among the oil producing cartels would continue to feed volatility and greed. The upward spiral of oil prices would continue indefinitely. Mark had concluded that future relief at the gas pumps would be temporary and unsustainable. The oil cartels, fed by their voracious appetite for ever-increasing wealth were determined to tease their captive consumers with brief price reprieves, only to quickly drive them up again and thereby setting new highs. These unscrupulous energy czars were intent on confusing the consumer into accepting that a temporary price reduction was a "bargain" in order to thereupon justify further increases. They had learned well from their MBA and marketing courses taught by professors in American universities. Armed with their "Made in America" knowledge and expertise, they invariably returned to their homelands to put into practice what they had learned. Talk about biting the hand that fed them!

How ironic that the preservation of Santius' very *status quo* that had been intended to prevent an erosion of Santius' stock price was now the reason why Santius' shares had dropped twenty-five percent in their value.

However, Mark Gentile did not feel vindicated by this turn of events. He was saddened that the company he had so loyally served for so long had failed to adopt his vision. There was no smugness, only regret that he, as Santius' past leader, had opted for passiveness in advancing his strategic plan. Perhaps, he was to blame in not more actively challenging the Board to adopt his strategic plan. Perhaps he had given up too quickly!

Had he acted as a true leader? Had he overstated in his mind the need not to engage the Board so as not to create a rift within the company? Perhaps, if he had challenged Cavendish publicly on his contrary corporate strategy; if Mark had clearly vocalized these differences, Santius may well have emerged a stronger and more unified entity with Cavendish and his followers set aside.

As Mark finished his coffee with these conflicting thoughts swirling in his head, he realized that it was only by completing the task he had abandoned or, at least, by repairing the harm caused by it, that he could finally put to rest the internal turbulence that had continued to take refuge in his soul since his resignation.

He wondered whether he might yet have an opportunity for personal redemption.

With these unresolved questions dancing in his head, Mark wished Marina a good day and set out to meet with Tony Ruprech to continue with their discussion on how Mark could assist in pulling Santius from its current predicament.

CHAPTER 30

The fruit orchards and vineyards on the slopes up from the Bradano Valley, however, knew nothing of the violence and civil unrest experienced in the Middle East and elsewhere. Activities here were dictated not by the oil cartels but by Mother Nature. There was no volatility to be found anywhere on the Basilicata wheat fields, vineyards, fruit orchards or olive groves. Man-fostered unpredictability was not a concern for the Lucani laborers.

The Acerenzesi's season of toil had arrived once again. There would be little time for television or gossip for several months hence. The days would be busy from early dawn until the sun's last rays had retreated for the day. Weekdays and weekends became merged and indistinguishable. The tasks of plowing, seeding, pruning and spraying were important tasks that would be governed by available daylight rather than the need for rest. Each season's necessities needed to be completed in time for the next round of activities in the seasons following.

Indeed, the Acerenzesi had become accustomed to interminable and intensive labor, from plowing the fields in late February until the last olive had been picked and converted into golden liquid in late November. There would be plenty of time to rest, to reacquaint themselves with family and friends and to generally reenergize the body and the soul from the Santa Lucia celebrations in mid-December until winter's grip was relinquished in mid-to-late February.

It had been thus for hundreds of generations. It would continue in this fashion for hundreds more.

CHAPTER 31

"Good morning, Mark and welcome back," announced Anne Marie at the Santius reception desk. "I'll tell Tony's assistant that you've arrived. Tony asked me to call up as soon as you got here." And then, with a smile and a wink, Anne Marie continued "I'm planning my first trip to Italy this summer and I hope I'll be able to lean on you for some advice".

Anne Marie had been employed at Santius for over twenty years—one of the most senior employees in the company. Respect for her was so well acknowledged throughout the employee ranks that she was one of the very few individuals who got away with addressing even the most senior and highest ranking executives by their first names, nicknames or surnames, depending on her mood of the day and on her personal relationship with the target.

Anne Marie was a spinster who chose not to marry, although it was well known that she had had a number of worthwhile suitors. However, her absolute honesty and her inability to suffer fools gladly had apparently scared off eligible bachelors. Anne Marie had once been a beautiful woman. Even now in her fifth decade, she was still a "stunner";

regrettably, though, an elegant and decisive woman who would likely never find a mate with the self-confidence to engage in a relationship that entailed accepting a woman with a mind of her own and who unfailingly was on a mission to assert her independence. Santius had become Anne Marie's life; its employees her adopted family. To her, Mark had always been "Mark"; Burton Cavendish, on the other hand, had always been "Mr. Cavendish" or, simply "Cavendish".

"Hi Annie, it's good to be back and to see you again. I'll tell you all the do's and don'ts of *il bel paese*, but I'll start now with one clear caution: it's about four to five pounds a week of weight gain", Mark said matter of factly, "no matter how conscientious and careful you are".

Annie's jaw dropped and, sensing her shock, Mark went in for the kill: "Just imagine: *cornetto al cioccolato* and a steaming *cappuccino* for breakfast; a plate of *Neapolitan paccheri* pasta sprinkled with delicious *pecorino* cheese for lunch; a *gelato* and iced *espresso* for a mid-afternoon snack; a *grigliata di frutta di mare* (an assortment of grilled seafood) accompanied by a mixed *arugula* salad with lemon juice and drizzled with extra virgin olive oil with shaved *auricchio* cheese for dinner, accompanied by slices of homemade *pizza bianca* baked fresh with rosemary and oregano spices; and, of course, a second *gelato* later in the evening as you begin the two-hour nightly after-dinner *passeggiata.*"

As Annie's tongue unconsciously gently licked her upper lip, Mark knew he had failed miserably in his attempt to tease her. "Sounds like these will be the most delicious ten to fifteen additional pounds I will ever carry around, Mark", Annie smiled as she pointed Mark to the elevator. "When do I start my first lesson?" she asked as the elevator doors closed before Mark could reply.

Mark was glad to be back at his home-away-from-home. His recent discussions with Tony about the problems Santius was now facing had energized him. He was looking forward to re-engaging in a role that could repair the harm inflicted on the company. He also secretly hoped that this eventuality could also fill the painful void that his departure from the company had created.

CHAPTER 32

On the third floor, reserved for the executive offices, Mark exited the elevator and turned immediately to the left into the main boardroom, the site of so many corporate battles, large and small, over the years.

As Mark entered the room, he noticed to his right his personal Inuit carvings he had gifted to Santius on the opening of its new offices; the whiteboard with its array of multi-colored markers on the far wall, the keepers of so many secrets, both strategic and financial, over the years; a small espresso machine on the corner of the walls, one of the few corporate perks Mark had allowed himself.

Mark felt at ease in this familiar setting. He was comfortable. He was secure. He was brimming with confidence, for no apparent reason.

Mark's momentary reverie came to an abrupt end when he was instantly surrounded by his friend Tony Ruprech, accompanied by the entire executive management committee, comprised of the five most trusted and senior executives of the company.

"It's good to see you and welcome back to your old digs", Tony commented, as he enthusiastically offered Mark his old chair at the head of the table.

"I wish this were totally a social gathering Mark but, as I have already explained to you privately, you will soon hear in more detail that there are momentous decisions that this company must make and our management committee has concluded that there is no one more able to provide advice and direction than you. I hope you'll agree to help us with our future strategies once you've heard our presentation of where things stand currently. Although I have already outlined to you some of the more serious events here at Santius, some rather dramatic issues have arisen over the last twenty-four hours that have added a dimension of new anxiety. Save for the executive management committee present here, no one else has any knowledge of the details you will hear today. The board of directors was generally advised by my memo earlier this morning and its chairman, Burton Cavendish, has called an emergency board meeting tomorrow morning, at which the entire board will hear the same details we are presenting to you now".

Mark was stunned by the atmosphere of panic that was palpable in the boardroom. But he didn't show it.

Tony, to his immediate right, and the other four executives, two on each side of the table, sat down facing the whiteboard. Tony rose, walked up to the board, faced the group and began his dissertation without notes and without the usual video props.

It was becoming clear to Mark that he would soon again be at Yogi Berra's "forks in the road", and that he would need to choose a direction that would likely be life-changing for him.

Adrenaline began to flow through Mark's veins; he put on his "game-face" and focussed all his attention on Tony Ruprech.

CHAPTER 33

"My friends", Tony began, "I have asked you to attend this extraordinary meeting to discuss the dramatic issues facing our company. I invited Mark to join us because we all respect his insight and his knowledge of the company, with the hope that he will provide advice and direction to us all". With this brief introduction, Tony set the scene for what was to become one of the most important corporate meetings in the history of Santius; a meeting that would lay out the groundwork for decisions that would determine the very future of the company.

Methodically, Tony began his presentation. From his old colleague's uncomfortable body language, Mark knew that Tony was about to reveal matters that were crucial to the company and possibly life or death to everyone of its employees and shareholders. With his shoulders sagging and his voice trembling, Tony dug deep and got ready to recount painful details that brought together the most senior officers of Santius in this unscheduled, emergency meeting.

"We are facing the most difficult challenge of our lives, both corporately and personally", Tony stated. Mark noticed that the glass of water Tony was holding in his left hand was now visibly shaking, with the danger that its contents would spill out. It was as if Tony Ruprech was now caught in a time warp that had caused his immediate aging, by the minute. It was an impressionable sight; one that added immeasurably to the gravity of the moment.

"Santius' bank, until now one of our staunchest partners, has formally put us on its urgent watch list", Tony indicated, much to the surprise of those assembled. Mark was particularly stunned because he had developed a relationship of trust and confidence over the past many years with the chairman of the bank.

Back in the days of the many uninterrupted positive quarterly earnings for Santius, Mark and Jonathan Fielding, the chairman of New World Financial, had become friends, often seen together at social and sporting functions.

Quite apart from their respective duties to promote their services and needs to the other, the two leaders had grown fond of each other personally. They each shared a character trait of transparency and honesty in the way they led their lives both personally and in business. Because they trusted each other, they always entertained the needs of the other quickly and with a minimum of formality. Negotiations were always brief and to the point. The two friends instinctively accepted the other's declarations and assumptions, knowing that each had offered the other the best final position possible, thus shaving off days of otherwise useless and frustrating posturing.

Jonathan had been the first external executive to offer Mark his regrets when he resigned from Santius. Unbeknownst to Santius' succeeding management, however, immediately following Mark's resignation, Jonathan had inscribed in the bank's file an emphatic note to the effect that, going forward, deeper scrutiny over Santius' financial performance must be undertaken.

Jonathan Fielding was now still chairman of New World Financial. The bank's notice to Santius of its being placed on the "urgent watch list" had been signed personally by him. New World's almost $150million of combined operating, revolving and product development lines of credit to Santius were deemed to be now at risk, in light of the company's deteriorating financial circumstances. As a result, Fielding had concluded that a more critical and continuous monitoring of Santius' operations was required to ensure that there would be no default in its regular debt payments. It was an extraordinary, cautionary edict that the bank had placed on all Santius' accounts.

Fielding had justified this action to himself and his board of directors by concluding that, after all, no bank wanted to make a call on the repayment of these massive loans. Such a drastic step would be taken only when, as a last resort, the bank felt that the continued viability of the company's operations was irreversibly at risk. Then, and only then, would the bank terminate the "partnership" with its client and become merely a lender that would seek only to protect its loans by legally enforcing the existing contractual covenants.

Jonathan Fielding had concluded that Santius had now reached such a critical stage that the bank's internal auditors and financial experts needed to review continuously Santius' operations and financial decisions to ensure that the lines of credit did not grow beyond the set limits.

The bank chairman had also instructed the bank's external legal experts to begin a review of all contracts between the bank and Santius and, particularly, the standard security agreements that existed between lender and borrower, by which all the borrower's assets were used to collateralize the loans.

While the chairman had not yet decided to "pull the legal trigger" against the company, he was nevertheless getting ready to step in to enforce the bank's covenants, both as a secured and an unsecured creditor, and to assume direct control, if need be, over Santius' assets.

The vultures were clearly beginning to circle over Santius. The financial decay was now becoming more and more visible.

Jonathan Fielding had personally concluded that, unless Santius implemented dramatic corrective measures immediately, it was only a matter of time before the bank's relationship with its long-standing client would be irreparably broken.

The bank chairman personally regretted how things had changed so dramatically over the past year. He had applauded Mark Gentile's new strategic direction for Santius a year earlier and had quietly supported his friend in this endeavor. It was regrettable that the company's board of directors had not had the courage, or the foresight, to break with the past and engage in a new direction that would ensure the company's future survival.

Following Mark's resignation, Jonathan Fielding had privately expressed to a number of his internal colleagues that he wished his friend Mark Gentile were back in the saddle to lead the company in what was destined to become an extremely tumultuous and dangerous journey.

Tony completed his presentation to Mark and the assembled senior managers and, immediately thereafter, asked Mark to join him in his office for a private discussion.

"Mark, we desperately need your help" Tony began. "The situation is much more distressing than I just announced to my staff in the boardroom. In fact, Cavendish privately told me earlier today that he has recommended to the board that we should try to reverse the dramatic downturn in revenues by implementing the very strategic plan that you had announced and that the company rejected at last year's shareholders' meeting."

Tony searched Mark's face for any self-congratulatory sign, but found none. Instead, he saw in his friend's features the look of a person who had clearly absorbed the gravity of the moment and who was now trying to find ways to lessen the company's impending doom and, with it, its shareholders' investments.

"This is a desperation move, and the market will see it as such. Santius has missed the last quarter's earnings and its revenue projections were 30% below estimate", Tony continued haltingly as his voice dropped to a whisper. "Mark when you announced your strategic plan and its intended conversion from fossil fuel to alternate energy sources last year, Santius was sitting on substantial cash reserves that would have softened the blow of reduced revenues. Now, the company has not only depleted its cash reserves but, as you heard earlier, our bank has put us on its 'watch list'."

Tony stopped for a moment, searching for his final comments: "Mark, Fielding has been a supporter of the company and a friend of yours for many years. However, Santius' recent revenues erosion has alarmed him. Jonathan has confidentially told me that he and the bank's board have lost confidence in our company and he is ready to call on the loans on the very first default on our loan payments."

Tony slouched in his chair and, seemingly defeated, he said: "Santius will barely make its next loan payment due next month even if we cut or postpone current expenses", but, in any event, we will not have sufficient cash to make the one after that. We have barely two months to show dramatic changes or the bank will irreversibly put the company "in play" so that Santius, as we know it, will forever disappear.

Mark listened to his friend's update in stunned silence. He knew that the bank's call on the loans would immediately spell the end of the company. Such a material event would require public disclosure. This, in turn, would serve to alert the executives and operations managers to jump off this sinking ship and seek out other employment. Further, this would provoke its suppliers to require cash on delivery for engine and auto parts and other essential supplies. Ultimately, all these events would serve to warn Santius' customers that the company was on an immediate downward trajectory that could lead to bankruptcy.

The domino effect would be swift and dramatic. The company could become insolvent in short order. Several billions of dollars of market value would be wiped out. As a result of the collapse of the stock, regulatory action would be instituted by hungry regulatory investigators seeking both a political benefit and a replenishing of their departmental coffers through the imposition of substantial fines.

As traumatic as this seemed, Mark knew that a regulatory investigation into the collapse of Santius' stock would only be the beginning of the challenges for the company, its executives and its board of directors. The next, and perhaps most painful, activity would involve the circling by class action attorneys over the remaining corporate carcass, by starting civil actions in the hundreds of millions, if not billions, of dollars against Santius and each of its senior executives, board members, auditors, legal advisors and anyone else closely, or even remotely, connected to the company. Since insurance coverage would fall drastically short of the damage claims, each individual defendant would be put to personal risk.

Mark knew that, although the stakes were now extremely high, they could be expected to grow infinitely more serious in the next few weeks.

Strangely, Mark felt exhilarated by the day's revelations. As grave as the situation seemed, his mind was focussed and the course of action to be taken seemed to him to be clear and determined. Nevertheless, despite the obvious urgency in what needed to be done, Mark rose, placed his hand on Tony's shoulders and emphatically announced: "I'll do whatever I can to help us ride through this turbulence, Tony. I need to get to another important meeting now. I need to go overseas for about a week. Let me think about all this and I promise that we will resume our discussions as soon as I return."

As Mark exited the lobby elevator and moved toward the exit doors, he winked at Ann Marie and exclaimed: "Your first lesson in everything Italian starts in a short while, Annie", he smiled in reference to her earlier unanswered question.

CHAPTER 34

Mark's important meeting that cut short the discussion with Tony and the company's senior managers that evening was a dinner date with Marina and Dior.

As Mark walked through the parking lot to his car, his cheeks were on fire and a thin layer of perspiration flowed on his forehead; this, despite the cold winds' stubborn persistence in refusing to allow the last remnants of late winter to retreat and seek out its well-deserved seasonal rest.

Somehow, Mark had the feeling that Tony hadn't fully levelled with him on the depth of the corporate troubles that Santius had attracted. Tony's presentation, while indicating that Santius was now in dire financial straits, didn't make any reference to any knowledge of the very significant and troublesome future legal repercussions that would most likely follow.

Mark's extensive legal and corporate backgrounds gave him the inescapable feeling that Santius would soon be on a downward trajectory that would put its continued survival in severe doubt.

CHAPTER 35

The table reserved for him at the far corner of Fabrizio's Ristorante had served as Mark's desk where transactions involving many millions of dollars had been inked. It was there, at that very table, where Cavendish and Mark had their last encounter that had ultimately compelled Mark to dig into the deepest recesses of his soul and force him to make his life-changing decision to leave his ambitions behind and search for a different, less materialistic existence.

As Mark entered the restaurant, he stopped inside the door and relived, for a few seconds, that entire episode: the one-upmanship Cavendish had played through his game of musical chairs; Mark's metaphorical ordering of "*pappardelle al cinghiale*" (pasta with wild boar ragu) and Fabrizio's delicious, but deliberately malicious, translation as "pig ragu" and his ambiguously flattering statement to Cavendish that the food item had been made especially for him.

Mark came to realize much later that Cavendish's greed and calculated arrogance were the traits that drove Mark to the conclusion that in order to have moral and ethical salvation, he needed to resign from Santius immediately. Indeed, Cavendish's personal greed had forced Mark to re-evaluate his own life and to decide that he had to choose a different lifestyle—one that eventually led him back to his homeland. It was in his hilltop native town of Acerenza where Mark sought peace in his mind and in his soul by re-living his childhood memories and finding the lost idealism of his youth.

Fabrizio's Ristorante had been the catalyst that drove Mark to search for, and finally find, his inner Marco. The establishment had long since been Mark's bridge to his homeland. Eventually, it became the invisible bridge from Mark the ambitious adult to Marco, the youth with virgin idealism.

"Hello Mark, it's good to see you again. You have two important guests waiting for you at your usual table", the affable Fabrizio grinned as he pointed to the corner table.

Marina and Dior rose in unison to greet Mark when he approached the table.

"Dad, you seem really preoccupied. Any problems?" asked Dior as she rose to greet her father with a tight hug. Mark had always marvelled at his daughter's powers of perception; how Dior could analyse a slight body movement or an almost imperceptible facial expression; how she could use her sixth sense, her inner feelings, to arrive at a conclusion that was invariably accurate. Mark and Marina had always felt that their daughter's special gift would serve her well as her career unfolded. Mark was desperately hoping that his daughter's innate intuition would allow her to avoid the land mines that she would certainly encounter in life's tortuous journey.

CHAPTER 36

It had been many months since the Gentile clan had enjoyed dinner together at Fabrizio's Ristorante. While the restaurant had been a second office for Mark, he had taken Marina and Dior there only occasionally for family dinners.

Sensing that this was a special occasion for Mark and his family, Fabrizio had donned his chef's attire to personally take over in the kitchen. As a result, he had announced to his special guests that there would be no menu that evening and that dinner would be exclusively "the chef's choice"—a popular custom in southern Italy where chef-proprietors would often make meals for their friends without the need of menus. These amiable restaurant owners were always at the ready to welcome their patrons to their establishments and to treat them as family.

"So, how did your meeting with Tony go, Mark?" Marina asked her husband, as she rested her chin over her upright fist. "Have things changed since you left . . . ? her voice showing concern.

Over the last year, Marina had been careful not to provoke her husband into a discussion of Mark's last few weeks at Santius. She was now sorry she had introduced this sensitive topic because she knew that the incidents with Santius' board and its chairman were still an open wound for her husband.

To be sure, Mark appeared to hold no grudges over the events that had led to the re-awakening of the moral and ethical principles locked away during the years of his ambitious climb to the top of the corporate ladder. Nevertheless, it was obvious to Marina that her husband had been deeply affected not so much by the end of his corporate life but by his regret that it had taken him so long to rediscover life's most important qualities: the pure idealism of one's youth; the importance of ethical values; the personal need to seek and find the joy of being satisfied with receiving no external rewards for one's actions toward others; and the realization that personal fulfillment is all that's really important and the only thing that is truly permanent in life's journey.

"Santius is in bad shape", Mark started. With this brief introduction by Mark, his two precious companions were now set to attentively listen to every word of Mark's description of the encounter. They both knew that Mark's future plans, and therefore theirs also, were totally tied to the degree of personal involvement he was to have in attempting to repair Santius' current problems.

"But as troublesome as Santius' problems are now, I have a very strong suspicion that they are about to become so serious as to put its very survival at risk, and to drag down with it the personal lives of many of the decision-makers."

Mark hesitated a minute, collected his thoughts, and continued: "Corporate issues give rise to financial problems. When that happens, legal issues normally take hold and drive down a company and its entire management team. In other words, Santius has now reached the second level of its problems. The final level of urgency, the so-called red alert, will soon surface and, when that occurs, it's usually only a short time before the downward slide starts accelerating".

Mark toyed with his glass of red wine, took a sip . . . "Why, it's Aglianico, it's our own wine . . . it's Santiana-Vino's brand that we're exporting to North America", he stated matter-of-factly, but with great pride.

From the half-opened kitchen door, Fabrizio smiled contentedly at seeing his friend's reaction to being served Mark's own wine from Acerenza.

CHAPTER 37

By the end of April, spring had finally perked up enough courage to make its debut in Eastern Canada. As Mark pointed his car toward Blue Mountain, a resort area a hundred miles north of Toronto where Mark and his family had their country home, the sun shone brightly. It was a mild early afternoon when Mark and Marina reached their mountain-side chalet. Deep feelings of nostalgia enveloped them as they opened the front door to what had been their second home for so many years—so many very important years.

Pictures of Dior adorned the walls in the family room—Dior skiing her favorite run, "Happy Valley", slicing down the mountain virtually at their back door; Dior canoeing down the Mad and Noisy Rivers; Dior swimming in Georgian Bay a few hundred yards to the west; Dior hiking along the Bruce Trail following its hundreds of miles through a serpentine route from the Niagara Escarpment up along Swiss Meadows and beyond; Dior on her 12-gear mountain bike, catapulting from the top of the mountain, zigzagging at breakneck speed down to the village at Blue Mountain where Marina and Mark would often wait for her, while soaking up the sunshine over a glass of white wine on the flowered patio at Copper Blues.

Unlocking their chalet's front door was like walking into the Gentile's personal art gallery and museum of family memories. Paintings of the four seasons were hung on every wall in the foyer, living room and dining room. Here, prominently on the main wall, a cherished painting of a downhill skier from the 1988 Calgary Winter Olympics gifted to them by one of Mark's dear friends. There, a painting showing the Village at Blue animated by skiers in the heart of winter. On the far wall, over the fireplace, a painting of a solitary sailboat, rounding the cape that had housed the white lighthouse with its double-tiered red tiled roof and still functional, always at constant attention to warn large and small watercrafts away from the dangerously-rocky shoreline.

Hand in hand, Mark and Marina exited to the mountain-side end of their chalet through the back door and ventured on the mountain slopes with patches of icy snow still quite prominent, but now with bunches of multi-colored wild flowers fighting for space with the snow.

"It's difficult to imagine that there are serious problems in our world", exclaimed Marina, "when we see this breathtaking work of nature", she continued philosophically. Mark didn't reply. No commentary was needed. For now the two long-time soul-mates preferred to become lost in the visual beauty of the mountain. They held hands like young lovers, and as they filled their lungs with the crisp, perfumed mountain air, they became mesmerized by the surroundings, as if seeing them for the first time. They stood there, motionless and silently, for a long time totally enveloped by the beauty of Nature's gift to man.

That evening, Mark confirmed to Marina what she had suspected all along, that he would accept the enormous challenge of helping Santius in its hour of urgent need.

A week later, they were on their way to Rome to celebrate with their friends some special events.

CHAPTER 38

The train ride from Rome's Leonardo Da Vinci Airport, or *Fiumicino* as the locals call it, to Naples felt longer than the two hours it actually took.

Mark was preoccupied with thoughts about Santius and what it would take to reenergize its moribund state. Marina's thoughts, on the other hand, flew toward the Town of Ravello where they were headed to celebrate with their friends Luca and Anna Moranni their thirty-fifth wedding anniversary.

At the train station in Naples, they boarded the "*Circumvesuviana*" train that would take them around Mount Vesuvius and into Sorrento in less than an hour. From there, they would pick up their own car that had been left parked in the train station's garage and head for their *villetta* in Positano. Then, after recovering from their jet lag, they would drive along the Amalfi coastline to Ravello for their friends' anniversary celebration. There, they would enjoy their friends' company for a few days before heading to Acerenza for the annual San Canio festivities.

CHAPTER 39

Even with his Italian DNA, Mark was constantly amazed at the precision with which Italian drivers aimed their two or four wheel missiles with total reckless abandon indistinguishably on the country's highways, country roads, city streets or even sidewalks.

It was part of the Italian culture, Mark often felt, that Italian drivers employ their new-age chariots not as a technological means to arrive at a predetermined destination, but as a way to show off their innate, competitive spirit. The vehicle is somehow incorporated into their very being so that the driver, man and machine intertwined into a semi-robotic humanoid alien, becomes an indestructible force that must, at the same time, be respected, admired, feared and despised. Or so it seemed.

How else does one explain the frenzied activity when an Italian driver gets behind the wheel aimed toward a favorite café or other gathering point where, in an amazing feat, he will transform himself from selfish road warrior to a gentle and charismatic being who, once out of his beloved two or four-wheeled armour, will sit with friends for hours enjoying his "*dolce far niente*"? This complete transformation is nothing short of severe and irremediable schizophrenia, built right into the psyche of most Italians. The fearless and indestructible humanoid, once off the road, capable of feeling, loving and showing all the sensitivities and frailties that are part of humankind.

Nothing shows off this self-proclaimed, mechanically-inspired prowess like that stretch of road from Sorrento to Positano, and then again from Amalfi rising to the crest of the mountain, on to Ravello.

This road is loosely called a highway, *S.S. 163*. In reality, however, it is a serpentine, narrow, two lane road, hugging the coastline, carved right into the mountain with no room to spare. No shoulders, and no widening, it simply follows the contours of the topography, mountains to one side and, on the other, the Tyrrhenian Sea three hundred feet below separated by mere inches.

Here, full sized Lancia's, Fiat Cinquecento's, buses full of terrified tourists and Ducati motorcycles all vie for space and for dominance, all hurtling around corners, twisting and turning at maximum speeds toward their personal destinations. All warping toward an invisible finish line that's always framed merely by the vehicle a few inches in front of them.

Today, however, the two adventurers had decided to take a detour off S.S. 163 to Marina del Cantone, a jewel of a fishing village with its only access being a solitary road partially asphalted into the original dirt path that, for centuries, had been frequented by sheep, goats, mules, shepherds and farmers.

Cantone's isolation in a protected cove spliced between two mountains was both its blessing and its hardship. It meant that at least once a month, Cantone's hardiest residents would need to take turns climbing the narrow road up the mountain, and then down again to Sorrento on the other side, to pick up necessary supplies that kept the Cantonese happy and self-sufficient for the ensuing thirty days.

Over the many years, the single road had been widened somewhat and, in stretches, some asphalt had been laid, almost as a "deposit" for future completion. But the completion of the road never came, despite repeated promises from the provincial Campania government and from the federal authorities.

It seemed that Marina del Cantone had been left behind by progress. This lack of attention ultimately became the very reason why it now enjoyed somewhat of a financial renaissance. Small bed and breakfast inns had sprung up at the bottom, carved right into the mountainside. Marina del Cantone had become a much sought-after haven by those seeking tranquility, whether to get away from the frenetic pace of everyday life in nearby Napoli or Salerno or from further away Rome, Turin or Milan. It had become a refuge for those who sought to find that ephemeral internal peace that one seeks, or to satisfy one's inexplicable yearning to get closer to nature.

Fortunately, even now Cantone had been largely neglected by foreigners, mainly because of its location some four miles up from Sorrento and then down to the valley below. This was a voyage not to be taken lightly: almost three hours of difficult zigzag navigation that could be undertaken only by those with a sense of adventure and even then, only by those with both patience and a strong constitution.

Mark and Marina had discovered Cantone quite by accident one day when they had decided to venture off the main road on their way from Sorrento to Positano. They swung left off the main road and soon were mesmerized by the rows of vines on both sides of the road; olive groves with their green nets laid under the olive trees ready to catch the olives as they ripened and fell to the ground. They were so taken by the beauty and peacefulness of the landscape that they decided to venture further and further up the mountain. No road signs and no signs of life. Only the lonely barking of a dog now and then to ensure that trespassers knew enough to stay away from the half-hidden farm houses further in from the road.

On this beautiful early May morning, Mark's Fiat had finally crested the mountain. Although with obvious fatigue, the small four cylinders had groaned continuously as the ascent became steeper. But, eventually, it made it to the plateau where the first and only directional sign pointed redundantly down the path to Cantone. Mark stopped the car for a moment and, with Marina, got out to savor the clean salted breeze as it wafted up the mountain from the sea. As far as the eye could see across the mountain and down to the bottom, farming plots had been levelled by laborious farmers to plant their vines, vegetables, oats and olive trees. Green was everywhere, save for the multi-colored hues of the sea that began with the light azure water by the shore and then grew to darker shades of blue out toward the horizon.

Mark and Marina got into their car and began the long and dangerous trek down the other side of the mountain. Long, because it would take them the better part of two hours to reach the village. Dangerous, because there were only a few inches of room dividing the road from the abyss. The descent was agonizing, with twists and turns dictated not only by the contours of the topography but also by the property lines of the various boundaries of farms and vineyards. "Unpredictable" was the best way to describe their journey.

"Did you hear a distant sound?" asked Marina as Mark's focus continued to extend exclusively to the next few feet of terrain ahead of them. "No" replied Mark, "what was it?" Just as Mark uttered these words, they both heard the unmistakeable whining sound of a bus horn from the next turn below. Seconds later, they saw a full-sized tourist bus coming at them, some twenty feet down, slowly inching its way up the mountain. When the two vehicles were within a few feet of each other, they stopped and waited. *A standoff,* Mark thought.

For a few interminable seconds, neither vehicle moved; neither seemingly willing to give an inch. Marina had warned Mark when they bought the Fiat that they should opt for automatic transmission. But no, Mark had wanted to show off his driving skills: "I used to drive a manual truck for the landscaping jobs I had during my university summers—I sharpened my teeth on much more difficult vehicles than this," he would brag. These small Fiats are a cinch. They are so manoeuvrable that they almost drive by themselves", Mark had declared to Marina but, secretly, also to the car sales agent. For no apparent reason, Mark felt he needed to be treated like any other Italian buying a new car. The question of automatic versus manual transmission would surely never arise with an Italian purchaser, and would certainly not be allowed to surface in his negotiations with the dealer now.

The door to the gleaming light blue bus opened and the driver came out. A short, pleasant-looking individual with a smile on his face and a friendly disposition. The bus driver's benign appearance emboldened Mark and he too climbed out of his car. Both gladiators walked the ten paces toward each other and when they were practically nose to nose, the bus driver announced with the usual Italian flare, pointing at his bus: "*Amico*, size really does matter in this situation. The rule on this road is that the smaller vehicle has to back up until it reaches a point in the road that allows the larger vehicle to pass".

This so-called rule had a ring of logic to it, although Mark doubted that it had been formalized into an actual "rule of the road". Nevertheless, Mark concluded that there was no other option and told his adversary that he would try to back up to let the bigger contestant squeeze by.

As Mark looked up the mountain, a sense of fear and panic gripped him. He neither saw, nor remembered, any widening of the road until the plateau at the top of the mountain at least a quarter of a mile up. Four hundred or so yards on that mountain, zigzagging backwards with a manual transmission Mark had not yet fully mastered, would be a gargantuan task.

Nonetheless, Mark, the brave soldier that he was, asked Marina to exit the car and wait on the spot while Mark put the gear in reverse. By now, most of the passengers on the bus had come out with their cameras ready to film the event. After all, this was not something they experienced every day. For Mark, however, his panic attack reached a new high. Italians are known as people who want to make "*la bella figura*"—want to look good to others—and Mark's DNA, although now mingled with a more stoic North American mixture of practicality and efficiency, required, indeed demanded, that he make "*la bella figura*". Nervously, as Mark gently squeezed clutch and accelerator pedals simultaneously, his Cinquecento groaned on his command, as if in protest. He was conscious of every inch of terrain gained, and desperately looked back through the side mirrors twisting his body back and forth to look through the back glass panel and the side mirrors to make sure that he avoided disaster by staying clear both of the downside edge of the road and the ditch on the other side. Twenty-five feet of painful backward progress and the spectators broke into cheers and rhythmic hand-clapping. Even Marina got caught up in the adulation of the crowd and began clapping and yelling "*Forza* Marco, you're doing great".

But Mark was not doing great. He was perspiring and totally overtaken by fear. His hands clasped the steering wheel so tightly that he was white-knuckled. His right foot played a continual dance between clutch and accelerator pedals. More than once, his indecision caused the otherwise obedient machine to stall.

Still, Mark persevered and inch by inch he progressed until he came to the first turn, one hundred and eighty degrees in the other direction. As Mark began to negotiate the turn, he looked in his rear view mirror and saw nothing but sea and sky. He froze into inaction. The spectators, now sensing adventure and drama, clapped even more loudly and became even more vociferous with their encouragement. Some, with their cameras ready, even walked with the car, exhorting Mark on. Of course, the effect was precisely the opposite for Mark. He desperately needed to show his self-confidence at the very time when panic overwhelmed him. It was essential that his fear not betray his intended stoic demeanor.

As Mark alighted from the car to check the distance to the precipice, the bus driver, sensing Mark's predicament, approached him and compassionately whispered: "leave this to me, my friend". He put his arm around his shoulder and asked Mark to stand aside.

He got into the car and intentionally stalled it. He turned the key again and again without engaging the clutch. Predictably, the car again stalled.

The bus driver came out, went to the side of the bus and took out his tool box. As he walked back to the reluctant Cinquecento, he yelled out to his passengers: "what do you say I help out our friend? His car needs a bit of mechanical work. Why don't you all take a break and enjoy a cold drink that you will find in the portable *frigo* at the side of the bus . . . and bring one for . . ." The driver looked at Mark and then, thumb to his own chest, he whispered "*Tommaso*". Mark quickly replied "Marco" and then pointing to his wife: "Marina". "Bring a drink for our friends Marco and Marina" ordered Tommaso.

The assembled crowd now sensing that the drama was over or, at least, would be postponed, rushed for the drinks and disbursed in groups to wait out the mechanical repairs.

Tommaso invited Mark to take the front passenger seat, started the car, and within minutes he had reversed the car two full turns around the mountain and into a ditch three hundred feet up.

Tommaso stopped the car and told Mark to get on the driver's side and wait there. Tommaso ran down the mountain, told his passengers, including Marina, to board the bus and, as he turned on the ignition, he announced "no wonder our friend was having problems with the car. Dirty spark plugs. These Fiats can be so unreliable sometimes. That's why I drive a German-made Volkswagen", and winked at Marina all the while.

When Tommaso squeezed his bus past Mark and his wounded Fiat, he turned off the bus engine and invited six of his sturdiest passengers to join him. A brief instruction to Mark and then the seven bulky men helped push the Cinquecento out of the ditch and back onto the road.

Tommaso went over to Mark, wished him and Marina well for the rest of the descent and told them, smilingly, that there were no more buses down in the village. Still smiling, Tommaso also told them that, as far as he remembered, there were only two other vehicles down at the base of the mountain and Mark need not be concerned because they were both motorcycles. "*Buona giornata*, Marco" and with a wave of the hand, Tommaso climbed back onto the bus to continue his upward journey, to the loud applause of his loyal followers.

"*Fare la bella figura*", Mark thought with a new sense of appreciation. When coupled with an act of pure altruism, it's a human trait that seeks to preserve another's dignity through an act of selflessness.

With the ordeal now over, Mark continued their descent toward Cantone, with a hint of wounded pride etched on his face. Marina looked straight ahead, her faint smile indicating she had more knowledge than Mark would have wanted her to have about Tommaso's helpful interjection.

CHAPTER 40

As had been promised by Tommaso, the rest of the descent to Marina Del Cantone was without incident, and without oncoming adversaries.

An hour later, Mark parked his car virtually at the water's edge and they walked over to Bar Titonno. This was a family-owned café, one of two in the small village. Mark led Marina into the establishment to offer their greetings to the affable owner Maurizio and then walked out toward the sea on the wooden platform jutting out over the shallow waters. The platform had a straw covering to protect Bar Titonno's guests from the hot sun, predominant even now in late spring.

With two glasses of iced tea, the two local foreigners enjoyed the splendor that nature offered them. Fishing boats gently bobbing in a sea of moving sparkling diamonds showing a changing lustre as the sun's rays penetrated the mild roll of the waves.

Mark looked up to his left as far as he could without ever seeing the crest of the mountain from which they had descended. To his right, was the placid Tyrrhenian Sea serving gentle lobs to the shoreline. Cantone's protected cove tamed even the most aggressive storms into a gentle lapping by the time the waves met the beach.

Further west, the color of the water and that of the sky lost their boundary, as the horizon totally merged sea and sky until the faint line totally disappeared, indicating that the merger had become complete.

Mark and Marina ate their freshly caught "*grigliata di pesce*"—mixed seafood grill—that Mark had ordered, with gusto. That little adventure coming down the mountain, it seemed, had given them an appetite that only Bar Titonno's generosity could quell.

As they finished their meal, Maurizio let lose his four cats to devour the remains. "Saves my needing to hire a server," he said casually as his unpaid employees cleaned off whatever had been left on the plates. "And saving you from buying a dishwasher" Mark replied with laughter.

After their goodbyes and promises to return soon, Mark and Marina settled into their car for the trip back up the mountain and then down the other side, to meet up with the main and only road leading to their adopted Positano.

The Cinquecento's small engine came to life with a roar. Marina seemed intent on discussing their forthcoming trip along the Amalfi coastline up to Ravello, but Mark heard not a word. He was deep in prayer that they wouldn't meet up with another oncoming vehicle, big or small.

The one adventure that Mark had experienced earlier seemed quite sufficient for one day.

CHAPTER 41

Two days of rest in their Positano villetta gave Mark and Marina the rest and energy they needed to get over their jet lag. They set out for Amalfi early in the morning and planned to arrive in Ravello by lunchtime.

Amalfi is approximately half way between Positano and Ravello and is where the road to Ravello, after a sharp left just beyond the bustling downtown port, begins to climb and continues to do so until, from a distance, the line of cars hoping to get to the top seems like a long reptile weaving in and out in one direction and then suddenly doubling back the other way.

Ravello is a nest at the top of the mountain. It is small in size and small in permanent population. In the months of June through September, however, the combined and temporary citizenry increases tenfold or more with wave after wave of gawking tourists making the pilgrimage to experience perhaps the most beautiful and spiritual site in all of Italy.

At almost four hundred metres straight up from the Gulf of Salerno, Ravello is a destination not for the faint-hearted. Ravello's famed magnetism is the stuff of dreams. It is an ancient town, built on a rocky plateau. There it sits majestically ruling, and at the same time dividing, the Valle del Dragone and the Valle dei Maiori. The only rationale for its existence is to provide to undaunted visitors the opportunity to admire the merger of the surrounding nature with its ancient culture and to allow them to admire breathlessly the picturesque towns down below lining the Amalfi coastline.

The winding around the vertical contours of the mountain on a narrow road with little to spare on the downward side, the upward-bound vehicles are forced to climb at somewhat more reduced speeds. Nowhere like the twelve hundred foot climb to Ravello can one distinguish the foreign from the Italian drivers. It is on this vertical topography that the locals show their fearless mettle. In and out, these miniature cars wind their way up at full speed, with the more patient drivers duelling a losing battle against the Ducati's, the Hondas and the Yamahas that zigzag at full throttle.

At the summit, Mark parked his Fiat in one of the lots just below Ravello's protective knee-wall, and holding Marina's hand, climbed up the winding staircase to reach Ravello's main piazza. From this vantage point, one could see the entire mountainside with its lush green slopes of vineyards hanging onto the precipitous cliffs, fruit trees and a variety of vegetables laid out in flat gardens carved horizontally out of the mountain.

Mark and Marina found a patio with a view in the piazza and, over a cold drink, admired the ancient buildings surrounding the circular square that had been laid out at the very crest of the mountain. The air was warm but with a crispness and purity that, mingled with the perfumed scents from the foliage and wildflowers surrounding the town, made this spring day an exhilarating experience.

After a few minutes of rest, Mark led Marina toward Via Santa Chiara to their destination, Villa Cimbrone, where they would stay overnight and where they would be meeting their friends.

As Mark and Marina entered the Villa, they were overtaken by the elegant beauty of yesteryear they encountered. Beautifully frescoed ceilings, glittering furnishings, priceless antiques lodged everywhere, even where one least expected them.

Once checked in by the elegant staff, they walked through the beautifully-manicured gardens admiring statues spread out throughout the perfectly designed lawns, each with its own descriptive history. Eventually, all paths in the gardens led to La Terrazza del'Infinito and Mark and Marina eagerly proceeded to the edge of the terrace. Only a four-foot steel fence separated them from the vertical drop of over a thousand feet straight down to the sea.

"I have read about this indescribable view from the terrace", exclaimed Marina in disbelief, "but this is beyond what anyone could possibly expect. It's beautiful and it's unforgettable . . .", Marina's words trailing off to a whisper, unable to do justice to the sight she was witnessing.

Indeed, with the early afternoon sun reflecting its rays from the lightly undulating rolls in the sea, Mark stretched his vision toward the far horizon—that faint and imaginary line separating sea from sky. That line that had now disappeared; it had welded together the two azure components of nature, to become one.

"It's easy to see why they have named this terrace *"La Terrazza del'Infinito"* Mark suggested, as he pointed toward the horizon. "There", he whispered, "is the invisible portal through which timeless infinity begins". They stared in the vastness before them for a long time, desperately trying to permanently etch the indescribable view in their minds.

As they turned to walk back to the villa to greet Luca and Anna and get ready for their celebratory dinner with their friends, Mark felt small and insignificant in comparison to the force, grandeur and expansiveness of nature. Even the biggest concerns and seemingly most insoluble problems devised by mankind now seemed trivial in front of God's outdoor Temple from which they had just emerged.

Santius and its whirlwind of problems had been quickly relegated to second place in Mark's mind, at least temporarily.

That evening, high atop the mountain, the four friends enjoyed a leisurely dinner on the patio, with only candles and soft moonlight providing guidance. They chatted, laughed and regaled one another with stories until late into the night.

CHAPTER 42

At breakfast the next morning, Luca and Mark reviewed the Profit and Loss Statements of Santiana-Alimentari and Santiana-Vino, Mark's food manufacturing and wine producing sister companies that Mark had formed in Acerenza during his initial visit just over a year back.

Luca, Marco's childhood friend with whom he had recently reconnected after many years of separation, had been placed in charge of both companies as a general manager of sorts. Luca preferred simply to be called "Capo"—Chief—by the almost seventy-five employees who now operated the two companies.

It had not taken Luca long to use his "smarts" acquired, first as a boy fending for himself in the streets of Acerenza, and later serving as its chief of police—as its "Capo". Barely a year later after taking on these executive roles, Luca could intelligently discuss a financial statement, could understand and deploy marketing strategies and, importantly, could draw up an expense and revenue budget on which Mark could fully rely.

Yes, Luca had made great strides in his business learning curve. He had become a very good and reliable executive. Luca had become more or less what he had earlier accused his friend Mark of being: "a big shot American"—at least, in the way Luca operated the Santiana companies.

Mark had been delighted with Luca's progress in the world of business and had so told him many times. It was now time for Mark to use action to reward his long-time friend and current business colleague. "Luca, this is an excellent update", Mark began as he sifted through the documents Luca had handed him. "We're making great progress with both companies. I never imagined that they would become profitable so quickly. More importantly, both companies are well run and you're the one responsible for that. Your days of being a police officer are over, my friend", Mark said jokingly, referring to Luca's old job in the town.

"Police Chief," Luca interjected mischievously but firmly.

Mark turned to the last several pages of the report containing Luca's recommendations for the future growth of the businesses and added: "Luca, I agree that our next phase of expansion into Asia, and particularly China, should be delayed until we have a more defined leadership role in our products within the areas we are now serving. China and India can wait a bit longer to savor our products; after all, they have waited thousands of years already . . . ," Mark winked as Luca broke into hearty laughter. "I agree with you that, while we wait for China's and India's wealth to be somewhat more distributed among their citizens so that they can afford to buy our Basilicata products, we should focus on consolidating those regions where Italian goods like ours are already well-known and enjoyed—countries like the United Kingdom, Germany, the Nordic Countries and Eastern Europe. After all, millions of their people already visit Italy frequently and have enjoyed our wines, our olive oils and our spices for years. These are easy targets for us. We don't need to convert them to our products. It's simply a matter of having them continue to eat our foods and drink our wines when they return home after their vacation in Italy."

Luca thought for a moment and then added "there will be plenty of time in a few years for us to expand our exports to the other side of the world".

As Mark concluded his thoughts, he noticed that Luca's earlier smiles had gradually increased and had now turned into a loud belly laugh. Mark was caught up in Luca's merriment and both laughed gregariously without any defined purpose, until Luca pointed to his report with his index finger and motioned to his friend to turn the page. And there it was, thought for thought, at times word for word, precisely the ideas Mark had just described. "You're a dangerous man, my friend", Mark scolded Luca amiably. "You're beginning to think like me, a dangerous trait for you to have acquired". Mark hesitated and, jabbing at Luca's arm with his index finger, he continues "soon you'll be promoted to Chief Executive Officer" Mark said with a grin, emphasizing the word "Chief" recalling the pride with which Luca had repeatedly told his friend that he was "Capo—Chief—of Acerenza's police department, although it was a well-known fact that in Luca's department Luca Moranni was chief of only one, himself.

Mark closed the report and the two friends now concentrated on their breakfast of freshly sliced oranges, toast and local cheeses. Over *cappuccino*, Mark told Luca the good news that he was making him a substantial equity partner in both companies. To start, he would grant Luca twenty-five percent of the shares of the main holding company that owned both operating companies. "This is for past "services rendered" Mark announced. "If you show the same commitment and results in the future, we'll have a similar discussion next year." Mark's brow suddenly furrowed and he instantly acquired his familiar distant look as if his mind was now travelling across the Atlantic at warp speed, ". . . but my transferring this ownership to you is not for nothing, as I suspect I will have a busy several months ahead in Canada and, during that time, I am expecting you to take the reins of control to an even greater degree to make sure that our companies will continue on their defined operational and financial trajectories", Mark placed particular emphasis on the word "*our*" to point out the newly-created joint ownership in the Santiana enterprises with his long-time friend.

Luca rose from his chair, hugged his friend and thanked him for his generosity. "You became a big shot in the corporate world, but you're still Marco where it counts: here . . ." Luca's voice cracked as he pointed to his heart. "I knew last night that you have unfinished business over there", Luca's hand waving across the sea, "but you can count on me to do my best in making sure that our Santiana-Vino and Santiana-Alimentari will continue to grow in prestige and value", concluded Luca with the kind of pride that only a substantial equity owner in a business can have.

Yes, Luca had indeed come a long way very quickly, Mark thought as he led his friend back toward the hotel entrance. Mark told Luca that he wanted to have one last look at the sea from the terrace and they agreed to meet at check-out an hour later.

At the edge of the terrace, Mark leaned on the banister and, as his gaze ran westward over the placid waters toward the distant shores of North America, he became reflective: "*Yes, Luca was the perfect example that education, knowledge and experience are not the only ingredients leading to success in business, and in life. Generosity of spirit, loyalty, commitment to an established strategy and hard work are the key criteria for success. These are innate qualities that can't be taught or learned. Everything else that's needed can either be acquired through schooling or experience.*"

Mark observed several fishing boats on the waters below returning with their nocturnal catches, bobbing gently as they approached the shores. Mark's thoughts refocused: "*Two friends with so much in common in the first half a dozen years of their lives were forced by circumstance to interrupt their friendship before each was able to, again by circumstance, renew their bonds. For several decades, each would pursue his destiny individually, separated by great distance. Each fulfils his own set of goals and objectives in very different cultures, a world apart. Somehow, though, fate merges their separate paths unexpectedly, when neither of them thought that their futures would again intermingle.*"

All the while, Mark continued to stare out into the azure expanse in front of him and once again became a philosophy student in a small classroom on the second floor of his college in University Circle. There, in those heady and caffeinated days when theory rather than reality ruled his life, Mark had become enthralled with the conclusion that man is governed by his own free will and determinism. The French philosopher Descartes particularly espoused the theory that man, and man alone, shapes his own destiny. That man is either the author of his own misfortune or that he alone should take kudos for whatever successes he manages to attain: Mark could almost hear his philosophy tutor: "*This long-held theory by many philosophers is attractive because of its simplicity. One has choices in every activity or omission in his life. From the simplest daily activities such as whether or not to cross the street, what foods to eat, what car to buy . . . these are all choices that man makes consciously realizing that his choices could have been different. Every such decision, every such choice is a conscious exercise of the mind. It is the mind's exclusive domain.*"

And yet Mark knew that there was a countervailing theory, one that is more mysterious, more spiritual, less logical. A theory that had become more appealing for Mark: "*It's too simple a conclusion to blame a reward or failure to the mind's process,*" Mark had felt. "*How do we explain that complex and vast knob of emotions that are guided not by the mind but by the soul? But then, what is it that guides the soul? What is the soul? No one, not religion, not philosophy, not science has ever attempted an adequate and concrete definition.*"

Mark had concluded years earlier that the best attempt to answer these questions had been made by religion in stating that the soul is all that's good in a being, but a "good" that's pulled this way and that by a larger and more complex force unaffected by the mechanical human mind . . .

Mark had, indeed, made conscious choices in his life. It had been his determined decision to resign from Santius after having considered the alternative. It had also been his decision to return to his native town where he had hoped to find that elusive balance in his life—where he could recapture the idealism of his now-distant youth. And yet, as explainable as these choices had been, Mark had not chosen to meet up with one-time friend Luca and had had no say in the resumption of their friendship. These were events superimposed in some other unexplained way. How to describe such superimposition had been the work of ancient philosophers and of modern-day university professors who used these complex enquiries and riddles to write unsolvable questions on test papers.

Mark had often ridiculed these so-called philosophy exams which served to wreak havoc with the student all the while containing questions that were impossible to answer and riddles that could not be unfurled: *"And so, because the human mind is more comfortable with the finite than with the infinite, these ethereal concepts have been branded with captions such as 'free will and determinism' or 'fate and destiny'. If humans were capable of concretizing the invisible force that often guides our lives, they might more easily grasp the fact that choices being directed by a mechanical mind may be too simple an explanation. Our actions, our omissions and our rituals may well be guided by the mind but our emotions, our happiness, our sadness, all those unexplained feelings that form part of who we are, the vagaries of the soul, are not explainable . . . except, that they are guided in each of us by a supernatural force that was always intended to remain a mystery."*

Mark broke his reflections with a start. He looked at his watch and realized it had been almost forty-five minutes since he had left Luca. He pulled himself away from the banister and headed up to his room where, he guessed, Marina was waiting, all packed and ready to leave. *"I'm not sure I had any choice in slipping into this internal philosophical debate"*, Mark whispered sotto voce to Marina who had no inkling of what had led to the comment. *"But it's good to see that all those years of business and law haven't totally eradicated all the vestiges of the idealism of my youth"*, he thought with a sense of satisfaction in still having the youthful passion to internally debate these impossibly complex and abstract theories that unconsciously form the makeup of humankind.

And so, high up a Ravello hilltop, on this glorious morning, Mark Gentile had once again become a single combatant in a sparring between his mind and his soul; between the explainable and the indefinable.

Expectedly, this bout had ended in a draw, to be resumed within the minds and the souls of millions of future philosophers in the millennia to come.

CHAPTER 43

Late April in southern Italy is a visual feast for the eye and a spiritual experience for the mind's eye. This is particularly so in the Amalfi Coast.

And so it was for Marina and Mark, as they began their driving adventure from Ravello down and around the tortuous hills overlooking the Valley of the Dragone, on this warm and sunny day.

With every twist and turn on the narrow road around the mountain, alternating vistas of lush vineyards, olive groves and fruit trees competed perennially with the azure waters of the Tyrrhenian Sea, far below.

Here and there appeared and disappeared small settlements, the villages of Minori and Maiori, interspersed with sloped fields of produce and untouched areas seemingly left intentionally untouched so that the artistry of nature could be left to play her artistic hand. Wild flowers of every imaginable hue were painted on a canvas that was briefly interrupted by a farmhouse or a patch of fruit trees, but that would then continue haphazardly to fill the canvas in different directions.

Down the mountain at a snail's pace, Mark's *Cinquecento* squealed, seemingly in pain, as its gears fought to have traction against the vertical axis of the mountain. Every few hundred metres of advance was met with gasps of incredulity on the part of Marina, as one spectacular sight was replaced by another, and then another, as they slowly headed down toward the base of the valley.

Mesmerized by the continuous parade of individual and constantly changing vistas she was witnessing, Marina whispered softly: "How is it possible to compete with these views? Nothing can do justice to what we're seeing and experiencing. It's so sensual."

Soon, they would arrive at the town of Amalfi for lunch, before continuing their journey home to Positano.

Their lunch destination was 'A Paranza' at Via Dei Dogi in Atrani, a village just east of Amalfi. A Paranza has been a favorite for locals and tourists alike for years. Its longevity and success are due to the simplicity of its cuisine and the local authenticity of its menu. The restaurant had been highly recommended by Luca who claimed that, aside from his wife's home-cooked meals, this was one of the best culinary experiences in the entire neighboring provinces of Campania and Basilicata. High praise indeed from an individual who preferred rustic to gourmet and simplicity to complexity in the food's flavors.

What can one say about Amalfi, the queen city of the Costiera Amalfitana, that hasn't already been said? Not as dramatic in its position as Positano or Ravello, Amalfi is nonetheless a romantic town with its toes in the sea and its upper spine firmly planted within the Monti Lattari.

Amalfi's docile constitution of today hides its rather unique, and somewhat turbulent, history. It had started as a small fishing village almost thirteen hundred years ago when it claimed independence from the Byzantine Duchy of Naples that had dominated the entire area including Naples and Sorrento, until driven out by the Longobards.

Following its independence, Amalfi quickly evolved as a city-state that eventually became Italy's first important maritime republic.

Eventually, northern Pisa invaded Amalfi and a combination of this ransacking, the equivalent of a present-day "tsunami", weakened ancient Amalfi until ultimately, a few years later, the plague of 1348 dealt a fatal blow to the city and its citizenry.

The once-proud and powerful Amalfi thereupon changed its stripes and resurrected itself as a sleepy fishing village, forever relinquishing its ambitions for power and prestige. And thus, it continued to survive for hundreds of years, without much noticeable change, until it again drew inspiration from its beautiful natural setting. Amalfi dropped its armor as a maritime republic and donned its regal mantel as Queen of the Amalfi Coast, a title it prominently holds, with little contest, to this very day.

Although the entire coastline from Sorrento on the north to Amalfi has towns, villages and scenery unsurpassed in beauty and style, nevertheless, it is Amalfi that has lent its name to this entire region. And for good reason.

Along Via Genova and Via Capuano, Mark and Marina walked toward Piazza Duomo, perhaps the heart of the ancient Amalfi of yesteryear. Everywhere one looked through the covered porticos of the narrow streets, the remnants of medieval life could be seen and felt. The covered passageway of Campo de Cinnamelis is the continuing witness to the ancient Arabic spice market from the days when Amalfi was a throbbing seat of Arabic silks, perfumes, carpets and spices.

A stroll through any of the narrow, and still mysterious, streets brought back the intrigues, love and power from the tales of the privileged who frequented the life of courtisans during the Renaissance period. At the other side of every street corner, one could expect to meet the characters of John Webster's "*The Duchess of Malfi*" as the characters engaged in their acts of lust and vengeance.

A total contradiction, thought Mark, between Amalfi's rather turbulent pedigree as a past seat of power and its present beauty as a simple, small town basking in almost perennial sunshine, with the protected waters of the sea gently lapping at its feet.

Twenty minutes after leaving Amalfi's medieval centre, Mark parked his car on Traversa Dragone, a few steps from their lunch destination.

On hearing that Luca Moranni had recommended the restaurant to Mark, Enzo, the amiable owner of A Paranza, welcomed his two guests and led them to the far corner of the simple trattoria. The thick wooden table had deep scars that seemed to provoke its patrons to imagine past intrigues of love and conflict. On the table was a bottle of mineral water and a chilled bottle of "*Ravello*" that, as he poured the wine, Enzo explained was a local dry Rosé with a pronounced violet bouquet that would be perfectly refreshing on such a warm day.

There was no menu in A Paranza. Total trust in the chef's abilities and culinary choices were implicit in this charming establishment.

As the two long-time soul-mates sipped their wine, Marina asked "Now what, Mr. Gentile?" she smiled, "I've rarely seen you as *spensierato*—relaxed—"It' s as if this is the lull before the storm", Marina concluded firmly, but inquisitively.

Mark thought for a moment, "Yes, we'll have to return to Toronto very soon", he began. "Yesterday, I received a phone call from Tony Ruprech. Remember Tony who was my chief operating officer and who was then appointed CEO of the company to replace me after my departure? I didn't tell you of this call at the time because I didn't want to interfere with our enjoyment of Ravello. Tony said the situation at Santius is very fragile. The company's bank is getting ready to call in their loan. And there are whispers of a regulatory investigation on the company's recent actions."

Mark was now deep in thought. His eyes were again distant, as they had been when Mark's internal turmoil had begun a year earlier. Marina was now sorry she had provoked the discussion, but was nevertheless anxious to hear the latest update from her husband.

"My concern, Marina, is not that any one obstacle can't be thoughtfully overcome. It's that the combination of events that are now merging may conspire to create a downward spiral for the company. When that happens, it may be very difficult to stop it. Greed and fear take over; rational thought is abandoned. That's when mistakes are made that can land a fatal blow. This is exactly where Santius is now. One false move and the company could quickly vaporize".

Mark's last comment was so emphatic that Marina became startled. She recovered quickly: "Serves them right for not following through on the strategy you had recommended, Mark", she replied in a show of support, but without conviction.

Their exchange was interrupted as a young server, likely a family member of the restaurant's owner, brought out a steaming large platter of "*scialatielli alla Paranza*"—homemade noodles with fresh seafood—as a *primo piatto*". The freshness of the simple ingredients titillated their taste buds. Although delicious, Mark and Marina had by now become experts in the pleasures of Italian dining. They knew that they had to pace themselves. Eating in Italy, and particularly in southern Italy, was a little like running a marathon. Although full of ambition and energy at first, the race always belonged to those who paced themselves properly so that they could cross the finish line in relatively good shape. With this in mind, the two diners intentionally left untouched half of the platter.

When the affable Enzo suspected that the *scialatielli* dish had run its course, he removed it and ceremoniously offered, hands stretched toward the kitchen: "*oggi, per secondo, offriamo polpetti in cassuola con i polpetti pescati stamattina stessa—today, for the main course, we offer a baby octopus stew in a clay pot, with the seafood freshly caught this morning*".

This last menu item was pronounced with such pride and formality that it demanded a comment. "*Benissimo*", replied Mark. "We know it will be delicious". Satisfied with this reception, Enzo disappeared in the kitchen, with a big smile on his face. Paying a sincere compliment is still the time-honored way of showing gratitude in Italy. It opens doors; it softens confrontation. It's part of the Italian psyche.

Over iced espresso, Mark and Marina shared a "*sfogliatella Santa Rosa*", an Amalfi Coast delicacy and speciality of A Paranza, made of a flaky pastry filled with sweet ricotta cheese.

Almost two hours later, after handshakes all around with Enzo and the young server, who by then had been identified as Enzo's niece, Mark and Marina left the trattoria and decided to go for a short walk to work off their lunch, before heading along S.S. 163, toward Positano.

Mark opened the passenger door for Marina: "This is indeed the lull before the storm, Marina". Mark hesitated and then continued, "I'm afraid that today is as carefree as it gets for quite a while".

He lifted his hand toward the sea and added "the storm clouds across the pond have gathered. The tempest will soon hit with such intensity that it may destroy everything in its path, and I'm not sure Santius can escape it."

As Mark shut the car door, he feebly said to no one in particular: "I'm going to try . . .", Mark's voice trailed off inaudibly.

Nonetheless, Mark's protective body armor was ready to be donned. The metaphorical battle lines were being drawn back home. Mark had been summoned to engage in one final battle. He knew that there was unfinished business to complete and that the quenching of his own internal turmoil could not be satisfied until he had put right the disastrous path Burton Cavendish had forced Santius to follow.

That distant whisper from across the ocean had, for Mark, now become an immediate cry to help an ailing friend. An urgent call to arms had re-awakened Mark into action.

Nevertheless, the inevitable corporate battles that were destined soon to begin would have to await a bit longer for Mark's participation. The next item on the Gentile agenda was attending the celebrations surrounding the *Festa di San Canio* in Acerenza on May 25th.

CHAPTER 44

On May 24th, Mark and Marina set out from their winter home in Positano for Acerenza to celebrate the San Canio festivities.

Although Mark's hometown was not particularly far in distance from Positano, it was nonetheless a long and tortuous drive across the interior of the Campania Region into neighboring Basilicata to the east. Once into Basilicata, the roads twisted and turned around hills and mountains and across valleys until the descent into the valley of the Bradano River, forever protector of Acerenza, and the final climb up to the town itself.

On May 25th, Acerenza, the sprightly old Lucanian lady, had downed her finery, put on her dancing shoes and got ready to party. Not just any party, mind you, but the most important event on the calendar.

While various other celebrations throughout the year such as the Santa Lucia festivities on December 13th, the autumn vendemmia and even Christmas and Easter carried their own important traditions, the annual celebrations of San Canio, the Protector Saint of the town, had its own air of importance. After all, this was the day when the Acerenzesi could celebrate their own Saint and thereby celebrate themselves.

The festivities consist of week-long events, beginning with celebration lights being installed throughout the main thoroughfares of the town and in the main piazzas. The celebrations are, at once, a religious festival, an open-air rock concert, a children's playground, and a gourmet's delight the likes of which are not seen at any other time of year. In short, it is a reason-perhaps, a wonderful excuse—to celebrate Acerenza itself, not simply the present, but also the millennia of its past history.

May 25th thus begins early in the day with a band parading the streets of the town playing both local tunes and classic overtures, and ends late at night with a rock concert in the Fossato and a midnight fireworks display.

It's already late spring in Acerenza, and the air is perfumed by the flowering fruits trees, violets and wild flowers on the sides of the mountain. The constant breeze flowing up from the valley envelops the town with a coalescence of perfumery not ever duplicated in modern-day commercial scents.

Beginning right after the afternoon meal-"*il pranzo*"—the air is energized by the shriek of children as they gallop away from their parents' grasp toward the series of long wooden carts lined up in and around the perimeter of the clock-tower square, simply known as "la piazza" by the locals.

As Mark and Marina inspected the various products sold by the vendors, Mark's memories reversed to some fifty years earlier when, together with his benevolent grandfather, little Marco, too shy to ask but all too eager to receive, would point to this candy or that toy with an indifference that unsuccessfully attempted to disguise Marco's real state of mind. Unfailingly, though, Marco's grandfather would see through this playful charade and, without seeing the need to ask his grandson, would buy him little "*torroncini*"—those concoctions of nougat and slivers of almonds blended together to form a chewy candy that Marco gleefully ingested in his mouth, much like a squirrel filling its oral cavity pouch with food to take home and save for the hard winter ahead. In spite of nonno's mild protestations to eat slowly, Marco's cheeks would temporarily deform his facial contours until his mastication caught up with his intake.

The late afternoon of May 25th was usually reserved for meeting friends and family, exchanging the latest news and gossip, and inevitably ending up in one of the cafes for a coffee or a cocktail. This particular day was no exception for Mark and Marina as they walked hand-in-hand from one end of town to the other, greeting friends on the way: "*Buona sera, Marco, ben tornato . . . auguri Marina . . .*" as they wound their way toward the Cathedral and circle back for another lap.

The two Canadians-temporarily-turned Acerenzesi had no particular agenda, no time commitments. They were there to enjoy the amiability of the people and to step back in time to when life was less frenetic, less complicated, more human.

After the evening mass in the Cathedral before a full house, celebrated by the Archbishop and several other priests, the exodus of the faithful began out of the church and onto the piazzale in front of it, with the statue of San Canio being carried by sturdy volunteers through the streets of the town and then back again into the Cathedral, all the while being followed by Acerenza's musical band and the adoring faithful.

Several hours later, the musical concert began, entertaining the young and the young-at-heart until the early hours of the morning, interrupted temporarily by the fireworks display at midnight. The fireworks lit up the black sky so brightly that they could be seen and enjoyed by the surrounding neighboring towns across the Bradano valley.

Even after the celebrations were officially closed for the night, the Acerenzesi were in no mood to stop their festivities. They lingered in groups chatting away or went to their favorite pizzeria for a late snack.

In the early hours of the morning, as the customary early breeze picked up in strength, Marina began shaking from the cold. "I better take Marina inside . . . after all, we Canadians aren't used to the cold winds of Southern Italy . . ." Mark announced, tongue-in-cheek, amidst good-hearted laughter by the group.

Another memorable activity in this magical town had been experienced, and for Mark, re-lived. Bit by bit, Mark's past life he had left behind many decades earlier was being reconstructed, one brick at a time.

As they got in their car late the following day ready to leave Acerenza, Mark smiled a smile of satisfaction and confessed to his wife with nostalgia: "this is the last of our relaxation for some time, sweetheart. The battles will soon begin back home. But I've never been readier to engage than now".

CHAPTER 45

Late in the afternoon three days later, Dior picked up Mark and Marina at Toronto Pearson International Airport. The flight over had been uneventful. Although a daylight traverse, Mark had uncharacteristically slept most of the time. His body was getting ready for activities that he knew would require his full and focused attention. There would be no respite until the task at hand was done.

As they set out from the airport, over Marina's gentle protests, Mark asked Dior to drop him off at Santius' corporate headquarters. Mark had a job to do. There was little time to waste.

On the phone while still in Positano, Mark had generally discussed with Tony Ruprech the pressing issues at Santius, although the specific details had been omitted. Just as Mark had predicted, Santius' revenues had dried up. As a result, its earnings forecasts were dramatically lowered by the company's chief financial officer. Analysts covering Santius wrote scathing reports. A selling frenzy began that sliced away two billion dollars of the company's market capitalization within three days. It seemed that the once darling of the stock exchange had now become toxic. Institutional investors couldn't wait to unload their stock, fearing continued slides in the share price.

Normally, when a company faces negative issues, an erosion in its stock price usually levels off after the more nervous and impatient investors sell their positions, and after the margin calls are satisfied to replenish the margin accounts. Then, demand usually starts building slowly by investors seeking to take advantage of the potential buying opportunity caused by the battered stock. This new buying demand, in turn, usually causes an uptick that can either be temporary, or more permanent if longer-term signs of optimism become evident. In short, analysts, investors and bankers look for clear signals pointing to a recovery before they will publish a report recommending an "outperform" or a "buy" on the stock.

The dire circumstances at Santius, however, offered no positive signals. The company's market niche had been totally eroded by the dramatically higher fuel costs. Every automaker, big and small, was now downsizing its cars, with smaller engines and lighter car frames made from aluminum or other light materials so as to lighten the weight and thereby offer better gas mileage. Every carmaker now also offered hybrid vehicles that further sliced consumption and drove up better mileage.

The very Santius fuel-saving strategies that, at one time, had been the envy of the industry, were now being adopted by the mainstream automakers, precisely because of Santius' proven past profitability. After all, with gasoline prices at the pump reaching five dollars a gallon, small had now become "*de rigueur*". Tails, chrome and fins were quickly disappearing in favor of marketing campaigns featuring small, zippy and colorful automobiles being driven by a fun-seeking and younger demographic. Gadgets were replaced by funky shapes and colors and by functional but cheap technology. Simplicity was now the new fad. Ostentation from size and luxury was being abandoned in favor of efficiency and practicality. One talked about "miles per gallon" rather than the amount of horsepower the engine offered. Even safety was being sacrificed at the altar of fuel efficiency.

In brief, it was as if Santius' original strategic plan formulated by its founder, the very same plan that Burton Cavendish had defeated, had been photocopied and sent off to every carmaker on the planet for immediate implementation.

This had been precisely Mark's fear. He had foreseen these events as inevitable. This is why he felt it was urgent for Santius to abandon its long-standing strategic plan in favor of the new, and admittedly more perilous, course of moving away from fossil-powered engines. Mark had become convinced that, if his fears materialized, Santius would not have the financial clout, nor the size, to compete with its more robust competitors. Mark had felt that if Santius did not quickly engage in partnering with an alternate energy company to draw up a new type of engine, the company would soon wither away and become redundant.

Mark's prediction of doom and gloom was now becoming a reality—much quicker than even he had earlier anticipated. Unfortunately, there was no place to hide for Santius or for its current slate of management and board of directors. Santius had little to offer; new technology seemed to have swallowed it whole. Lack of financial muscle prevented it either from competing using the old fossil-fuel model or from engaging in the new model of hybrid engines. "Small" was the new measure. The recent "cross-over" phenomenon, that happy medium between an SUV and a sedan that had taken over a big segment of the market for a while, had now quickly faded into obscurity, all as Mark had feared and predicted.

Had Santius followed the plan Mark had announced eighteen months earlier, Santius would have had the choice of partners, at a time when no one else was looking. Like at a teen dance, a delay, even a slight delay, in choosing your dance partner could inevitably cause the procrastinator to spend the rest of the evening alone, without a dance partner.

Regrettably for Santius, all the eligible candidates were now not only paired up but were actually on the dance floor. Santius was left on the sidelines and, much like a defenceless teenager, was now wondering why it hadn't had the courage to walk across the dance floor and choose its partner—the pick of any partner—before the first musical note was struck. It was easy to muse over what Santius could have become if only Burton Cavendish had placed on the backburner his personal agenda and accompanying greed.

On seeing Santius' financial performance and disturbing future trends, its analysts began to circle like hungry vultures. Out they came, report after report issuing a series of negative predictions on the future of the company. Gloom and negativity were everywhere within Santius. The one-time darling of the automobile industry had now become toxic. The same investors, individual and institutional alike, who at one time eagerly lined up to purchase Santius' stock now scrambled on who could push the "sell" button first.

There is often a fine line between success and failure. More often than not, emotion rather than reason governs one's actions. But not in the case of Santius. The evidence as to its incompetence was in; the trial was over. All that was left was the oncoming final verdict from the jury, its investors. A heartless jury devoid of compassion and set not to give a second chance but, rather, on jumping the queue to sell so as to salvage as much as possible from the quickly-decaying carcass.

CHAPTER 46

When Mark entered the Santius' boardroom, every board member was present. As well, the five-person executive management committee led by Tony Ruprech, was also in attendance. The tension in the room was palpable. Nervous faces were sitting around the long conference table, not knowing what to expect, but knowing that they would be in for a life-changing exercise.

Tony sprang to his feet and rushed to welcome back his old friend. Mark made his rounds around the table to greet every attendee. Mark recognized virtually everyone as either individuals he had hired or persons with whom he had worked during his recent tenure as Santius' CEO.

"Hello Burton", Mark offered his hand to Cavendish. "It's great to see you again. You haven't changed a bit". Tony and a number of others smiled subtly at Mark's facetious remark. "Yes, Mark, the board and I asked for your temporary input at this time", Cavendish lied.

Tony had, in fact, earlier told Mark that Cavendish had been the only dissent at the joint board/executive management committee when Tony Ruprech brought a motion that the company request Mark for his immediate assistance at this time of need. When it had become obvious that Cavendish was alone and ostracized in his dissent, he quickly retracted his dissent vote to make it a unanimous resolution "for the good of the shareholders" for whom Cavendish repeatedly had stated he was their protector.

"Well, Burton, thank you for your vote of confidence in me and I'm ready to assist the company in any way I can". More smirks all around, and this time less subtly delivered. This reaction around the table was a clear signal to Mark that Burton Cavendish had lost his hold on the board and that this group would take its current and future responsibilities seriously, without undue influence from Cavendish or anybody else. Cavendish's slumping upper body also confirmed for Mark that Cavendish's personal powerbase and influence had vanished. It was clear to Mark that Santius' current predicament had created a far different environment from that he had experienced more than a year earlier at the shareholders' presentation when Cavendish's cockiness and greed were at their pinnacle. Indeed, today's Cavendish was a beaten man, a mere shadow of the self-confident and powerful dictator Mark had encountered at Fabrizio's Ristorante where Cavendish had successfully manipulated Mark to resign from the company.

How the mighty have fallen, Mark thought for a second, as Tony Ruprech called the meeting to order. Sitting in isolation at the head of the conference table, Cavendish fumed as Tony robbed him of his mandate as Board Chairman.

CHAPTER 47

The corporate secretary distributed agendas for this extraordinary meeting.

Tony Ruprech rose and began his presentation. "Ladies and Gentlemen" he began, "I will first provide a brief status report on the current corporate events. After my presentation, we will adjourn for dinner that I've catered in. We will then resume our meeting with a full discussion. Mark and I have agreed that we will not end this meeting until we have agreed on a full plan of action. Tonight, we decide. Tomorrow, we start implementing under Mark's leadership, assuming we all agree on our new leader and on the plan he will be presenting."

Mark had never seen Tony so vigorous and so unafraid. It was obvious to all that Burton Cavendish's power and role had totally disappeared. Even more dramatic was Cavendish's total silence. Cavendish's position as chairman of the board had been reduced to one of title only. These unexpected and catapulting events had forced him to abdicate his role in substance.

Tony then proceeded to outline the latest events that had created the dire circumstances that had compelled the urgent meeting. "Our company cannot survive in this current environment", Tony began, "the Securities and Exchange Commission has now formally notified us that Santius is under investigation for its press releases issued some months ago in which the company declared that it saw neither operational nor strategic clouds on the horizon and that it foresaw continuing earnings growth and therefore increasing free cash flow from its operations". Tony paused for effect, slightly turned toward Cavendish, and continued: "the main issue that the SEC is probing is whether this was an appropriate corporate guidance given the board chairman's express knowledge that the then CEO of the company, Mr. Mark Gentile, had retained the most preeminent consulting firm to conduct a thorough review of the company's future strategy and that both the consultants and management had jointly concluded that Santius' existing strategy would lead to destruction if the board did not immediately change its direction".

Tony's words were like daggers piercing right through Cavendish's heart. Everyone in the room knew that the blame for the company's current predicament lay at Cavendish's feet. The members of the board now felt embarrassed that they had been so easily influenced by their chairman to unanimously agree with his recommendation to stay the ill-fated course. Upon belated reflection, each board member was now ashamed they had not had the personal courage to challenge Burton Cavendish's personal view that the shareholders' interests would best be served by continuing with the same strategic direction that had ensured past profitability.

Tony then pointed at Mark and concluded his remarks: "I now turn the meeting over to Mark because there are various legal and corporate ramifications that Mark is better able to explain". With that simple comment, Tony sat in his chair, frozen into silence by the overwhelming chain of events that had been unleashed.

Mark rose to address the meeting. He quickly surveyed the assembled executives and board members and noticed that his gaze was met with warmth and anticipation.

"Hello my friends", Mark began, "no matter how dark things seem at times, there's usually a way to avoid disaster, if one acts quickly, honestly and with determination". Although there wasn't a sound to be heard, one could feel loud sighs of relief from everyone around the table. The expectation in the room was that Mark would deliver a thoughtful and premeditated plan that would avert falling over the precipice both corporately and personally.

"There will be some considerable turbulence ahead both corporately and for some of the individuals in this room", he paused, and then continued, "however, we must all work unselfishly for the interests of all the shareholders of Santius rather than for the protection of any one person's individual interests". These brief comments served to provoke quiet reflection by everyone over his own particular conduct during the previous few months. There was now palpable anxiety and confusion on the faces of most of the audience. Seeing this, Mark felt the time was ripe to strike at the heart of his first, and possibly most important, recommendation.

Tony added more drama to Mark's last comments by calling a brief recess in order to allow Mark's introduction to sink into the consciousness of everyone, especially the consciousness of Burton Cavendish.

CHAPTER 48

With almost military precision, exactly twenty minutes later, Tony called the meeting to order.

Mark had noticed that during the break, small groups had formed outside the conference room with board members in one huddle, some members of management in a separate circle and the executive committee in a distinct grouping. Each group seemed intensively in discussion but without any interaction whatsoever among the various groupings.

By contrast, at the far end of the table, Burton Cavendish sat alone, in total isolation. During the entire recess, no one approached him. Clearly, Cavendish had been ostracized by the very groups of loyal followers over whom he had once carried large doses of influence.

In witnessing Cavendish's ostracization by his board during the break as a carrier of contagion, Mark could have been forgiven for perhaps feeling a sense of personal vindication in seeing how his one-time adversary had been humiliated. However, he felt neither vindictiveness toward, nor pity for, Cavendish's current plight. He had more important things to worry about than succumbing to emotions that, if allowed to have traction, could well derail his plan to save the company.

When everyone was again seated, Mark resumed his commentary: "I have carefully reviewed the SEC's formal notice and it is quite clear that the regulatory agency is investigating the company's disclosure statements made by our chairman, Mr. Cavendish, following my resignation as CEO".

As Mark brought back into focus those past events, Cavendish had had enough finger-pointing. He rose and loudly proclaimed "The disclosure statements that were issued were accurate and factual. There was nothing misleading in them. There was nothing improper. I will fight tooth and nail to protect my personal integrity . . .". Cavendish had put all his energy into this brief outburst. His face flushing with rage, he slumped down in his chair, his chin resting on his navel.

"And you may well decide to fight the SEC to the end, Burton, if that is your intention. However, this will have to be your personal legal fight without participation by the company".

Cavendish now flushing with built-up anger and seemingly reenergized, rose again and declared: "Mr. Gentile, this is exclusively a corporate issue. The company will obviously call me as its witness in laying out its defence. But this is Santius' problem and not mine, and not of any other board member. It's the company's legal obligation to defend itself and those of us who were in a supervisory role" concluded Cavendish. In laying out his position, Cavendish hoped that his comments would have the dual effect of distancing himself from the oncoming problems of the company and of influencing his board members to consider their individual legal risks and to vote to have the company carry the legal and financial burden of any defences that needed to be mounted.

To Mark the lawyer, it was clear that Cavendish had sought, and obtained, legal advice on the issue of his personal liability. Cavendish had obviously also received legal advice that he should record his position at the earliest opportunity into the formal records of the company for future reliance.

Mark calmly continued unaffected by Cavendish's self-serving statements: "The fact is that the SEC has indicated that it is investigating not only the company's disclosure statements but also Mr. Cavendish's conduct in suppressing from such statements any reference to the company's report received from its consultants that drew a fundamentally contrary strategic and financial picture than that painted by the statements he had signed and allowed to be disseminated to the public". Mark did not want to waste more time on this, and concluded "I believe that the company and Mr. Cavendish are in conflicting positions and I am therefore recommending that each of Mr. Cavendish and the company be separately represented by different legal counsel throughout the SEC investigation."

Mark stopped for a moment to see how his listeners were accepting the news. He saw faces that appeared apprehensive over the sudden escalation of these issues, but who also appeared to be resigned to allow their resolution to Mark.

Sensing that there seemed to be general confidence in him, Mark continued: "Also, to further avoid this obvious conflict between the company and Mr. Cavendish from continuing, I am recommending to the board that it immediately request Mr. Cavendish's resignation as chairman and as a board member and that if he refuses to resign voluntarily, a vote be taken among the remaining members of the board to seek his dismissal".

Mark then explained that the corporate by-laws allowed for the resignation or termination of any board member for cause and for the immediate appointment of a successor. Mark further indicated that the conflict between Cavendish's personal position and the company's eventual legal stance would likely be at odds so that it was best to prevent an aggravation of the conflict by allowing the chairman to continue in his current leadership role, or indeed, any role in Santius.

Cavendish's expression was one of shock, anger and utter humiliation. His eyes lit up like a raging inferno, but he said not a word.

Mark went on to recommend that the company agree to advance payments for Mr. Cavendish legal representation but only on Cavendish's strict agreement that if the SEC made any finding of wrongdoing on his part, or if any settlement were reached with the SEC in which Cavendish accepted the SEC's findings of impropriety against him, Cavendish would be obliged to reimburse Santius for the payments advanced for his legal defence. As permitted by the corporate by-laws, rules that had been signed by Burton Cavendish himself as chairman, Cavendish would be required to pledge all his Santius shares to secure this contingent liability for the monetary retainers to be advanced to him to pay for his legal expenses.

The board, together with senior management, unanimously voted to accept all of Mark's recommendations but, expectedly, with only one dissent.

Tony called for a second recess to allow Cavendish to consider whether he wished to resign voluntarily or to force a vote for his removal.

In a desperate attempt to salvage his personal downfall, both financial and corporate, Cavendish requested the rest of the board members to stay behind and caucus with him.

For the next several minutes, Cavendish could be seen involved in an animated discussion with his colleagues. Cavendish seemed once again to be the ringleader. The others, their heads bent over, apparently listening.

A few minutes later, Mark noticed that Burton Cavendish quietly slipped away through the exit sign that led directly to the rear parking lot.

Burton Cavendish's participation in this critical meeting had come to a premature end.

CHAPTER 49

After a few minutes, the meeting was again called to order. During the recess, the corporate secretary had taken the initiative to put Mark's recommendations into a formal board resolution that he quickly handed out to everyone: "Carried", announced Tony Ruprech, "and our collective thanks to Mark for having accepted the board's invitation to become its new interim chairman to hold office until the board election at the next corporate annual general meeting."

Mark sat in his chair and the bitter-sweet memories of the events in the last few months came flooding back. His seamless transition from the world of litigation law to that of corporate CEO; the trust and confidence his mentor, Gordon Welsh, had placed in him by hand-picking Mark to succeed him as a leader of the company Gord had founded; Gord's selfless act in choosing to spend the last few weeks of his life teaching Mark all he could to ensure Mark's success; and Mark's disagreement with Burton Cavendish's self-centred strategy of maximizing personal profits for purely personal gain rather than engaging in a process that would more likely guarantee long-term success for Santius and all its shareholders, including himself.

Mark Gentile, as the new interim chairman of Santius, rose and asked the corporate secretary to note in the minutes Burton Cavendish's unannounced departure from the meeting. Mark then added, now in a softer and more conciliatory tone: "Some of you may have attended Gord Welsh's funeral where I repeated Gord's oft-stated personal philosophy that success is important but only if it comes with fairness and integrity; otherwise, the price is too high." Mark had the undivided attention of everyone in the room. "These were Gord's criteria. These are the personal traits I inherited from him. These will be the underpinnings that I will ensure will govern Santius' activities going forward—especially now, during these very trying times when every action we take, or fail to take, will be scrutinized and judged."

Mark spent the next two hours outlining his intended plan of action. He spoke confidently. It was clear that he was now acclaimed leader in charge of Santius' destiny.

The next few weeks would determine whether it was too late to pull Santius back from the edge of the precipice. Nevertheless, the era of Burton Cavendish's self-aggrandisement and of personal financial greed had thus come to an inglorious end.

It seemed that, months after Mark had decided to relinquish his corporate tenure and engage in his internal odyssey in search of life's most treasured mysteries an unexpected lifeline had been thrown to him; an opportunity for personal redemption; a final chance to quieten those internal demons that had been gnawing at his soul over his decision to quit and run.

Mark was determined not to fail this time. He knew that his internal journey would not be complete without clearing this final hurdle.

CHAPTER 50

The Enforcement Division's offices of the Securities and Exchange Commission in downtown Manhattan were, as usual, a hive of activity.

As Mark exited the elevator, he was greeted by three SEC officials, a young zealous-looking attorney, a securities expert and an accountant. Mark had, instead, come alone. He felt that as the newly-appointed chairman, untouched by the allegations of wrongdoing that had swirled around the company, he had a level of credibility that didn't need bolstering. Besides, Mark had figured, the SEC would have certainly done its research and would know that it had been Burton Cavendish's devious mishandling of Mark's corporate strategy that had been the foundation of SEC's intervention. The company's decision to remove Burton Cavendish as chairman of the board, the apparent wrongdoer, and to replace him with the untainted Mark Gentile would add both to the credibility of the company and to the ability of its new chairman to steer it out of continuing trouble with the regulatory authorities. Or, at least, that was what Mark hoped.

The SEC trio welcomed Mark warmly and thanked him for his initiative to discuss the "extremely serious" issues at this early stage of their investigation. They proceeded to a small internal office furnished simply with a wooden table, six chairs, and a vintage black telephone sitting on a mismatched walnut credenza. On one wall was a picture of the SEC crest; on the opposite wall was hung a picture of a smiling President Obama—a smile belying the gravity of the issues that were routinely discussed in that meeting room.

"Mr. Gentile, thank you for coming in", the securities official began. "It's not often that a corporate wrong-doer takes an initiative to want to discuss matters this early in an SEC investigation".

Before Mark could reply, however, the young zealous attorney interjected: ". . . early in the investigation yes, but not so early for us not to have arrived at an initial view that here we have both corporate liability on the part of the company and also personal liability on the part of its chairman, Mr. Burton Cavendish". With this ready-made conclusion, the SEC attorney stared intently at Mark, hoping to provoke a response.

Mark had represented a number of clients in regulatory investigations during his days of legal practice. He knew that, to some extent, these aggressive opening statements had been scripted to inculcate into a target the clear notion that any early negotiations with the SEC would be difficult and protracted. After all, Mark knew that the SEC had coffers to fill with potentially large fines, in addition to its genuine desire to prevent unscrupulous companies and executives from skirting away from rules and regulations intended to protect the public.

"I wanted to come in early and discuss with you gentlemen how we may better cooperate with you and assist with this investigation", Mark stated matter-of-factly but with a sincerity that was immediately recognized and appreciated by the trio. "I'm not here to get advantages from you, but if your research has reached the point where we can discuss next steps, then we should perhaps do so, even at this early stage. Regardless, I can pledge the company's full co-operation during your investigation."

The over-zealous attorney had been constantly shifting body positions in his chair from the start of the meeting, Mark had observed. This was a sign that showed his eagerness to add a notch to his prosecutorial belt at the earliest opportunity. Mark knew that joining an enforcement office of a powerful regulatory agency was usually a temporary tenure for many young and ambitious lawyers. It would be a rite of passage for them to get as many convictions, through trials or consents, as quickly as possible so that within a few short years, their *curriculum vitae* would be brim with financial recoveries through court-imposed levies, or through consents. Armed with these achievements, they would then join powerful law firms to ply their trade to now defend the very targets and the very conduct they had once despised and driven into submission. This seeming schizophrenia was a well-worn path followed by most young and ambitious attorneys, so recognized both within and outside the Agency.

Mark's reflective analysis was broken by the attorney who, without conferring with his colleagues and without so much as throwing a glance their way, offered: "I am ready to proceed, Mr. Gentile. I have already drafted a 'Wells Letter' to be issued in a few days. I am sure that, as an experienced attorney and long-tenured senior executive of a listed company, you fully understand the repercussions of such a letter to its intended targets". *It was customary for regulatory agencies investigating serious crimes to avoid names and, instead, to debase them with the simple but pejorative word "targets",* Mark observed.

Mark knew very well that the issuance of a so-called "Wells Letter" normally came when the Agency had concluded that it had sufficient evidence to convict. The effect of the letter was intended to indicate the likely charges against the targets and offered them a brief window of time to attempt to disprove the contemplated charges with any additional evidence of their position. The mere receipt of a "Wells Letter", however, was a dreaded occurrence because it was considered a material event within legal, accounting and auditing circles. As such, it required public disclosure. Almost immediately following such disclosure, there would normally result frantic selling of the stock with a precipitous drop in stock price.

These catastrophic repercussions following the disclosure of a "Wells Letter" occurred because the investors and analysts covering the company unfailingly accepted such "Wells Letters" as clear indications of guilt, that the Agency had fully investigated the issues and that it had concluded that there was sufficient evidence to convict and to extract from the company very substantial monetary penalties and, possibly, jail time for the personal wrongdoers.

Neither institutional holders of large stock positions, nor analysts covering the company, nor individual investors would wish to hold equity in a company that the government had targeted as criminal and that was managed by unscrupulous managers. And so, the selling frenzy would begin, and sometimes continue, for a number of days. It was not unusual for such victim to lose up to fifty percent or more of its market capitalization, that is, of its entire value, in a matter of days, or even hours. The SEC well knew the cascading effect of its "Wells Letter" on its target, and often used it as not only a true indication of its internal position in respect of the investigation, but also as important leverage to extract substantial negotiated penalties very early in the investigation.

"And the 'Wells Letter' that I will issue, subject to approval from the Enforcement Director, will refer to several counts of illegality against the corporate target. It will also contain several counts of illegal conduct on the part of the company's chairman, Burton Cavendish—including the exercise and sale by him of several hundreds of thousands of corporate options almost immediately following his presentation to the company's shareholders, a year back".

The legal zealot stopped for effect, and then continued with a delicious smile on his lips: ". . . any idea, Mr. Gentile, why Mr. Cavendish would sell out his options position immediately following his statement to the shareholders that the profitability of Santius would continue indefinitely without interruption? One might have expected a contrary behavior on the part of Mr. Cavendish, unless . . . well, unless he was sitting on information, unavailable to the public, showing that he didn't believe his own expressed optimism".

The legal zealot was now in his glory. Like an eagle flying mercilessly toward its defenceless victim, he was now unstoppable: ". . . so we looked for the 'smoking gun', Mr. Gentile. And guess what we found? We discovered what you already knew—that a thorough report from Merkson, the consultants you had engaged, showed that unless Santius immediately changed its strategy, it would very soon be squeezed out by . . . how did you phrase it, Mr. Gentile . . . 'rendered irrelevant by its more corpulent competitors'".

Not bad advocacy skills for a young attorney, Mark thought. A little rough around the edges, perhaps, but that would be cured by a bit more experience. However, his research had been impeccable and his method of presentation, although somewhat over-dramatic, was effective. Indeed, Mark concluded that the legal zealot would make an impressive figure before a jury trying this case. He would also make an attractive hire in a few years by a large and successful midtown law firm.

The attorney continued: ". . . so, either Mr. Cavendish was suffering from a severe case of dementia in selling out his options position just as he was singing the praises of a company that was in line for higher profits for the future, with a resulting higher stock price . . . or he didn't believe the story he was advancing to the shareholders".

With a victorious twinkle in his eyes the attorney continued: "If Mr. Cavendish truly believed what he told the shareholders at the meeting, he would have preserved his equity position for a soon-to-be increased stock price. On the other hand, if this was a carefully constructed scheme by Mr. Cavendish to spew out optimism to his unsuspecting audience while believing quite the opposite, then it all becomes very clear that this was a gigantic fraud perpetrated by the Chairman of the Board on his company and on its defenceless shareholders."

The attorney, took a long sip from his water bottle and began to lay out his theory: "Mr. Cavendish, in fact, strongly believed that the change of strategy you and Merkson had recommended was inevitable, just as you did, Mr. Gentile. However, his personal greed propelled him to fear that its announcement could immediately spark a selling spree by disgruntled shareholders who would now be asked to park their expectations of continued corporate profitability and to accept, instead, a lengthy postponement of the historical quarterly profits. But Mr. Cavendish, given his age and also his prior corporate history, didn't have time to wait until the changes took hold to reap his profits from the sale of his stock. He decided that he couldn't afford to wait the few years that were needed for the corporate rebound. Nor could he take the personal risk that the stock might not rebound. So he decided to cash out now when the price was high rather than wait until your new strategy took traction."

The legal zealot seemed to become more animated and more energized as he prepared himself for the final kill: "Mr. Cavendish's plan included bolstering the stock price so that he could sell his position at inflated prices. This is exactly what he did."

The young attorney knew the script by heart. Throughout his presentation, not once did he look at his notebook nor at the large, unopened binder sitting in front of him, ominously titled ***Key Inculpatory Documents-Cavendish Prosecution***. "The irony, if there is one, is that our target totally agreed with your recommended strategy, Mr. Gentile. This is why, at the meeting, he spoke with an air of optimism for the company's future. Unfortunately, his criminal behavior lay in then contradicting his own expressed optimism by selling to some of the very investors who were unknowingly buying his shares. This was malicious and illegal. This Department is eager to present our case to a jury made up of reasonable men and women to rule on Mr. Cavendish's crime."

Having just gone through an effective "dry run" of his opening statement to the jury, the attorney benignly leaned forward toward Mark and concluded "For your sake, Mr. Gentile, you did the right thing by resigning almost immediately after Mr. Cavendish aggravated his already-criminal conduct by attempting to coax you to renege on the strategy you had set out to your management team, to the Board and to the shareholders. It was part of Mr. Cavendish's strategy to get you to come around to his own timelines to allow himself the time to sell his shares calmly and without hurry. When you refused to go along, his alternative option was to get you out of the company as quickly as possible, not by firing you—because that would have raised issues and would have immediately depressed the stock price—but by forcing you to resign."

The attorney then took the unusual step of rising, offering his hand to Mark and proclaiming: "Mr. Gentile, we know that you resigned without severance and without claiming any benefits continuation. It's not often that my colleagues and I see executives who sacrifice their personal financial advantages to do the right thing. Our Agency compliments you for that, Mark".

This was the first time during the lengthy presentation that the legal zealot had warmed up to Mark and had called him by his first name. *A hopeful sign*, Mark thought.

As the factual matrix had been released bit by painful bit, Mark was shocked by the depth of Cavendish's maliciousness. It now seemed that his only strategy had been exclusively motivated by personal financial greed. He had wanted to keep the *status quo* at Santius so that he could calmly dispose of his shares within a sea of corporate optimism, so as to maximize the receipts from the sale of his shares. He had wanted to sell out quickly when things were on an upward trend while, at the same time, trying to keep the positive corporate earnings for as long as possible so that when the axe fell, as inevitably it would, sufficient time would have elapsed to wipe away his trail of criminality.

CHAPTER 51

Regrettably for Burton Cavendish, the legal zealot had unraveled the entire *imbroglio* impeccably.

He had ended his uninterrupted soliloquy with the conclusion that Cavendish had not been suffering from any mental disability. Rather, he had consciously conceived a scheme to profit personally to the exclusion, and at the expense of everyone else, and with information that he had not made available to the public. The attorney then concluded: "In this office, we call that insider trading of the worst kind. It was not just 'garden variety' insider trading, mind you. It was not simply a matter of profiting from confidential and material information not communicated to the public. It was all that, plus the creation by Cavendish of false and malicious information so that he could not only profit but would also allow for the desert winds to wipe clean his filthy tracks".

CHAPTER 52

Mark asked for a recess, feigning the need to receive an important phone call. In reality, he needed a few minutes to regain his composure and to determine how to terminate this discussion in a way that didn't involve a full capitulation by the company. Mark had been stunned by the attorney's description of the evidentiary matrix that would be used against both the company and its chairman, Burton Cavendish.

Without knowing what the SEC had in mind but mindful of its attorney's parting comments about Mark's conduct at the end of his tenure as CEO of Santius, Mark was hopeful that the meeting might end on a positive note for the company.

Twenty minutes later, the meeting resumed. "Mark", the attorney continued in a tone more conciliatory and less adversarial, "you took the initiative to come in and see us at a very opportune time. A week later and it would have been too late. The 'Wells Letter' would have been issued and you would have been too busy in your corporate attorneys' offices trying to piece together a strategy to save the company from its financial doom". With the slightest hint of a smile, the attorney continued "but to your credit, you approached us just in time. That's two for two, Mark. So far, you're batting 1000". Mark seized on the inference created by those words as a hopeful sign.

"Our two key witnesses, if this proceeds to trial, ironically, will be you and Merkson, the strategy consultants you retained. Our case is simple. The evidence will be uncontradicted . . .", and, now winking at Mark, "I believe we have a very credible witness whom the jury will conclude has an outstanding ethical fiber".

Mark probably ought to have been flattered by the legal zealot's words, but his mind was too busy determining how to respond. The attorney, however, had other ideas. "We're ready to discuss a deal with you that will be open for acceptance only for one week. We will hold off issuing the 'Wells Letter' for this period of time to see if a settlement between us is possible. But before I tell you what we have in mind, tell me, Mark, whether you are here representing both Santius and Mr. Cavendish?"

Mark knew exactly what he was being asked and where the attorney was headed. If he was acting as agent for Cavendish, he would be conflicted from discussing any matter that could place the two SEC targets, Santius and Cavendish, in a potentially adversarial position. Mark replied quickly: "I am here exclusively in my capacity as chairman of Santius. In fact, at the recent board meeting where Mr. Cavendish was removed as chairman, I made it clear, and it is so recorded in the Minutes of the meeting, that Mr. Cavendish should get his own attorney and that neither Santius nor its legal counsel would in any way act for him personally".

Upon hearing this disclaimer from Mark, the SEC attorney, now a much calmer and friendlier legal zealot, responded with a smile: "Good, your batting average remains perfect. Let's break for lunch. There's a quick deli downstairs. Can we agree to resume our meeting here in thirty minutes? That will give me time to make a few calls"

Mark sat alone in the deli, biting slowly on his cheese sandwich. He felt a sense of optimism that he couldn't quite justify in concrete terms.

Nevertheless, Mark had a feeling that Santius' issues were moving ahead toward a resolution much quicker than he had anticipated.

Mark arrived back in the meeting room with five minutes to spare. Exactly thirty minutes after the recess, the now-affable legal zealot accompanied by his disciples, reappeared.

They sat down for what was to become a marathon session that would define Santius' road to fiscal salvation, or its path to eventual oblivion.

A full six hours after Mark had first arrived at the SEC offices, the meeting adjourned for the day.

His head in a daze, Mark exited the building and became lost in a multi-directional throng of humanity that was lower Manhattan during its daily rush-hour. His mind now throbbing with a mixture of exhaustion and anxiety, Mark picked up the pace around the human obstacles and headed toward the downtown Marriott where he was booked to spend the night.

CHAPTER 53

Later that evening, Mark sat in his hotel room, emotionally drained by the day's events at the SEC offices. He had ordered room service, but had merely toyed with his dinner. He was overtaken by wave after wave of thoughts, some flowing into his consciousness with focus, others ebbing away unresolved.

Mark's main strategy was to save Santius at all costs. The SEC intervention was the first and most difficult obstacle to overcome. Without a successful resolution of the SEC investigation, Santius' bankers would step in and formally call the repayment of its massive loans. Santius' equity value would substantially melt away and whatever value was left would be divided by unsecured creditors, including the legal sharks who would soon commence massive class actions on behalf of concocted Santius shareholders. These actions would most likely be started immediately after the SEC announced its preliminary conclusion of corporate guilt through the issuance of the feared "Wells Letter". Mark knew that he had to avoid the "Wells Letter" at all costs if there was to be any realistic chance of saving Santius.

Mark called Tony Ruprech at home. "Hello Tony, sorry for calling you so late. I'm still in New York. I've had a long meeting with the SEC". Tony interrupted his friend: ". . . are you over-nighting in the Big Apple, Mark?" Tony asked, knowing that the company's charter plane was at the Teterboro private airport across the Hudson River in New Jersey, at Mark's beck and call.

"Tony, today's events have unfolded much more quickly than anyone could have anticipated. It started out as a standard 'get to know the players and the issues' meeting, but it almost immediately evolved into an evidentiary presentation by the SEC and then unexpectedly evolved into an aggressive threat by them. Eventually, this led to a long settlement discussion". Mark stopped for a moment to let the news sink in.

Tony heard this initial shocker with absolute silence. Mark then continued: "As the SEC officers disclosed more and more of the evidence they had accumulated, it became clear that their principal target is Burton Cavendish personally, rather than Santius. In fact, they believe that the company, its management group, its board and its shareholders were all duped by Cavendish's self-interested strategy to cause the board to disseminate fraudulent statements relating to the company's future well-being. The SEC showed me proof that Cavendish withheld material information about the company even from the other board members".

Mark then went into more detail and explained to Tony that the SEC had concluded that, while they were prepared to settle the proposed charges against Santius, they would nevertheless proceed with formal criminal and civil charges against Burton Cavendish with a view to extracting convictions that would force a full disgorgement of the almost seventy-five million dollars in stock and sale of options profits Cavendish had reaped in the last year. Mark indicated that the SEC was also seeking a stiff jail sentence.

Mark further explained SEC's position that if a settlement with Santius was not reached, the SEC was prepared to proceed against both Cavendish and the company and would seek joint fines from both, in addition to a jail sentence for Cavendish.

"Tony, the SEC is prepared to drop all potential charges against Santius and immediately announce the end of its investigation against our company, on two conditions: first, that Santius will pay to the SEC one million dollars as a reimbursement for the SEC's costs and expenses for their investigation . . ."

Tony broke his silence: "What's the second condition, Mark?", he asked sheepishly, ". . . that I agree to testify voluntarily on Santius' behalf against Cavendish. The SEC wants a written statement confirming that I hired Merkson to do the strategic review for Santius and that both Merkson and I disclosed to Cavendish all the details, interviews, financial data and market research supporting Merkson's report and recommendation to the company. The SEC doesn't really expect from me more than the truth of what happened, Tony."

Tony started to respond when Mark continued: "Oh, and the SEC also wants my confirmation of the reasons why I resigned as CEO of Santius. The SEC is apparently placing great importance on what they say was Cavendish's manipulation in either forcing me to capitulate on the strategic plan I had introduced, or to effectively resign from the company. It's part of the SEC's theory that Cavendish acted maliciously and with full deliberation in wanting me out of the company so that there could be no internal interference with his personal plan to enrich himself at the expense of the company and its remaining shareholders".

Tony was shocked by these revelations. After a few seconds, he asked: "Mark, did you accept these terms? How long do we have to consider their offer and potentially finalize an agreement?"

Mark reflected for a moment and then replied "I neither accepted nor rejected their conditions, Tony. We have a week to sign a deal. If we don't do a settlement by this time next week, the SEC will issue both to the company and to Cavendish a formal 'Wells Letter'. That will be when there will be an accelerated and unstoppable domino effect on our company, its operations and, ultimately, on its ability to survive."

Mark stopped for a moment and then concluded: "Tony, if we don't settle before the SEC's 'Wells Letter' is issued, the company is as well as dead. Formal criminal charges will then be laid; the bank will pull the plug on all our loans; the stock price will dive to insignificance; and the plaintiffs' attorneys all over North America, both north and south of the border, will start massive class actions that will go on for years or until the company declares bankruptcy".

Tony was quick to reply: "Mark, with the picture you've painted, we don't seem to have much choice, do we?" Then Tony added: "You're the chairman, Mark. We have given you full authority to represent the company and do what you believe to be in its best interests. We have full confidence in you, but to me at least, where we have to go seems pretty clear: We need to settle and the sooner the better." And then, Tony graciously added: "Mark, if you feel you need my personal support, you have it in whatever direction you believe is best for the company".

Mark thanked Tony for his vote of confidence and ended the discussion by telling him that there were still important items on the wording of the proposed agreement for him to discuss with the SEC the next day. As an example of the tasks ahead, Mark knew that the wording of an agreed press release coming from the SEC was crucial to how Santius would be perceived by its investors, its bankers and the analysts covering the company.

Mark was exhausted. He would turn in early, but he knew that he was in for a sleepless night.

CHAPTER 54

A full agreement between the SEC and Santius was signed two days later, after the completion of some rather aggressive negotiations between Mark and the SEC's legal zealot on the precise wording of the proposed announcement of the settlement. Each side had tried to extract from the other its perceived advantage in the deployed semantics. Neither wished to create the misimpression that the other side had won.

Mark knew, from his extensive legal background and experience in negotiating innumerable settlements, that the best settlement was one where neither party was totally happy with its results. A good settlement was always one that allowed each side reasonably to save face.

One day following the completion of the settlement, the SEC released the following brief press release:

"As previously announced, the Securities and Exchange Commission commenced an investigation into the alleged misconduct of Santius Corporation and its Chairman, Mr. Burton Cavendish. Following an extensive review of all its available information, the SEC has decided to

cease its investigation into the conduct of Santius Corporation. The SEC is, however, continuing with its investigation into the alleged misconduct of Mr. Cavendish."

Mark could not have hoped for better wording. The most difficult point of the negotiations had been Mark's insistence that there be no mention of Santius' agreement to pay one million dollars toward SEC's costs of the investigation. Mark knew that the class action attorneys would be dissecting every word and innuendo in the SEC's press release to determine if there could be detected any expressed or implied indication of a finding of guilt against the company that they might use to launch class actions against the company on behalf of willing, and even unwilling, Santius shareholders.

Mark was quite satisfied that no such detection existed, or could even be inferred, from the public announcement.

CHAPTER 55

Mark's first stop following the SEC's formal press release was at New World Financial, Santius' main bank.

He was greeted warmly by its chairman and long-standing friend, Jonathan Fielding. After exchanging personal greetings for a few minutes, Mark informed Fielding of the recent settlement with the SEC. "Mark, we are really happy to see you back in the saddle at Santius. Issues were developing very quickly and, to be honest, until your arrival, we were spending most of our days with our lawyers and accountants, analyzing our loan and security agreements, getting ready to pull the plug". Fielding smiled and apologized that all the bank's efforts and expenses in retaining their professional advisors were now destined to go to waste: "No worries about pulling any plugs," Mark replied, "Santius will once again rise from the ashes and become the profitable auto-maker it once was".

The chairman rose, shook Mark's hand, and said:

"Mark, it's good to hear that. Getting the SEC to walk away from laying charges was a major win for you and the company".

Mark thought for a second and then said simply: "There really wasn't any evidence of wrongdoing on the part of Santius. The SEC did a pretty thorough review and finally decided that the company was not at fault. It's to their credit that the Agency agreed to let us out early without further pain and suffering".

And with that last comment, Jonathan Fielding pledged his bank's support and wished Mark well in the attempted corporate resurrection.

CHAPTER 56

As usual, Fabrizio's Ristorante was busy for lunch this Thursday. Fabrizio welcomed back Mark, winked at him and led him to Mark's usual table at the far end of the room. Sitting at his table was a solitary man, head bowed.

Burton Cavendish seemed to have aged years in the last short while. When he saw Mark approaching, he rose and as Mark approached the table he motioned him to sit at his customary chair. *No playing "musical chairs" this time*, Mark thought.

"Burton, I have little interest in having lunch with you today. Why don't you just tell me what you have in mind. I'm pretty busy these days".

Cavendish seemed unsettled by Mark's bluntness. He had the look of a desperate man. "Mark, what deal did you strike with the SEC? What's your explanation for the timing of the SEC's settlement with Santius and the reaffirmation by the agency of its intention to go through with charges against me personally?"

Mark replied matter-of-factly: "the timing of those two events was not my doing. I have no control over the SEC and I have no influence either over their prosecutorial decision or over the timing of their announcements". A deep sense of satisfaction ran through Mark's emotions, knowing that his nemesis had quickly learned of Mark's settlement with the SEC.

Burton Cavendish rose, his entire body shaking from anger. Pointing his trembling finger at Mark, he yelled out: "you don't fool anybody, Mr. Gentile. Santius walks away clear and I get nailed with all sorts of criminal charges? Both announcements are made back-to-back and you're trying to make me believe there's no connection between these two announcements? You sold me down the river, Mr. Gentile, and I hope you can live with that. Everything I did, I did for all the company's shareholders. I personally benefited, yes, but only as a shareholder of the company".

Cavendish turned his back to Mark and, as he walked away toward the exit, he half-turned toward Mark and warned him: "You haven't heard the last of this, I guarantee it . . .". Cavendish's tone was unconvincing, and his anger seemed to be directed more at himself for having been caught than at Mark Gentile for having succeeded in extracting Santius from any wrongdoing.

In spite of Cavendish's threat, Mark knew that the once great Burton Cavendish, former social climber and past candidate of the "Billion Dollar Club" was now a beaten man who would be known for his criminality and who would be living the last years of his life in personal disgrace. *"One works so long and hard to acquire a reputation, and it can all be lost in an instant"* mused Mark, as his thoughts meandered back to the lessons on virtue and ethics he had originally learned from his grandfather in his native Acerenza—the same principles he had strived to apply to his career and personal life through the many years that followed.

Sensing that Mark perhaps might need some moral support, Fabrizio came over and sat with his friend. He called over one of the servers: "A plate of *pappardelle al ragu di cinghiale*" for each of us. This is a time for celebration", Fabrizio said smilingly in obvious reference to the lunch Mark had ordered for Cavendish that fateful day, seemingly an eternity ago, when Burton Cavendish' arrogance and greed forced Mark to re-evaluate his entire life and caused Mark Gentile's life to change forever.

CHAPTER 57

"Friends, welcome to this special shareholders' meeting", Mark announced to the crowd.

The auditorium was standing-room only. Mark recognized many loyal faces in the audience. The atmosphere was tense with anticipation.

"My name is Mark Gentile, your interim chairman of the board. Many of you will remember me as your company's former CEO. The company and you as its owners have gone through a lot of turbulence lately, but I'm happy to say that we are busy overcoming our problems. I want to provide you with a status report of our successful actions over the last three weeks".

With help from the large screen erected at Mark's side, he explained clearly, and without spin, that Santius' bank had given its full support to the company and its entire management team; that the SEC issues had been totally resolved with the agency's agreement to abandon its investigation of the company and its prior disclosure statements. Mark added that the SEC was, instead, proceeding with charges against the company's former chairman, Burton Cavendish, including serious charges of insider trading. Not a sound could be heard in the room, as Mark reported on these events in a factual and understated manner.

"The most important news I have for you this morning, however, is that our board has ratified a major partnership agreement your company has signed with a significant alternative energy company to jointly develop state-of-the-art flex vehicles that will accommodate different types of energy such as electric, ethanol, natural gas and traditional gasoline. Our new partner and will soon undertake with Santius a round of public financing to raise sufficient funds to complete this development. We foresee these new cars coming off the assembly line within two to three years. And that's not all. Our partner is also developing a new type of cell battery to accommodate longer-distances for electric cars . . ." Mark saw relief and smiles among Santius' supporters in the room.

"As I said a year ago, the time of gasoline-driven engines is coming to an end. Not tomorrow or the next day, maybe, but very soon. The world has changed forever. More and more, consumers like you and me, will be demanding clean, safe and reasonably-priced engines powered by alternate energy to power our vehicles and run our industries. The contamination of our planet has become a concern not just for leftists and environmentalists. The environment is now a politically sensitive issue that will govern political strategies until we dramatically reduce our emissions . . .".

Not a sound could be heard in the large auditorium. Everyone's eyes and ears were focused on Mark and his speech. ". . . We are more and more becoming concerned about leaving our planet so that our children and grandchildren will inherit clean air and environmental safety. And that's a good thing. I intend to have Santius—your Santius—become a leader in this space. We will bring your company to a level that will once again make you proud of being the owner of a company that's profitable but that also cares for the environment in which it carries on business. The two concepts of profits and environmental sensitivity are not at odds with each other. They can live together, side by side".

The audience rose as one with this last comment. They cheered and applauded, putting their full support behind their company's new venture. Many in the audience recognized this last comment as part of the original strategy that had caused Gordon Welsh to found the company.

Mark stopped for a moment to measure the reception of his new strategic plan. He saw smiles and relief on the faces of the assembled investors. Mark motioned for the audience to take their seats and then concluded: "Your company is resuming the strategic direction your management team attempted to introduce a year ago but that was never implemented", Mark said with satisfaction. "We are now determined to see it through. We will soon return to our historical profits. All I ask for is your understanding and patience. If we get that from you, we are confident that we will all benefit in the future."

As Mark finished his speech, the shareholders again stood and applauded loudly.

Following the meeting, Mark felt invigorated by the reception he had received. He was full of optimism for Santius' future. In a quiet moment of reflection, Mark concluded that while this strategy should have been introduced at that time, nevertheless, it wasn't too late to repair Santius' current problems.

Mark's premature surrender to Burdon Cavendish a year earlier now seemed to be distant. *It's all up to me, now. No excuses and no one to blame,* he thought.

Mark was exhilarated by the prospect of repairing the harm for which he had assumed some responsibility in causing the company. He felt as if time had stood still, patiently waiting for him to resolve his internal odysseys and resume the reins of control. *Is this a lifeline to my personal redemption?* Mark wondered as he exited the auditorium.

At the opening of trading the next morning after news of Mark's speech had been aired in the media, Santius' stock rose almost twenty-five percent in value. *A vote of confidence from the equity markets,* Mark thought, as he savored the moment.

CHAPTER 58

The public offering to raise Santius' share of the funds needed for the joint development of the alternate energy project Mark had signed with its partner was going well. "At this rate" Mark reported to the board at their monthly meeting, "we will be substantially over-subscribed—that is, we will have more money than we need. It's a good barometer for the market's confidence in the strategy we announced".

What a difference a few weeks had made to the attitude and morale of the Santius family. From the top executive in the company to the delivery clerk, there was evident a newly-regenerated pride to work for a company that was on a path to success. "Our founder, Gord Welsh", Mark continued "would have been proud to see what we have accomplished, and would be particularly proud to see a continuation of that fearless, entrepreneurial spirit that so well defined Gord, the man".

Mark then motioned to Tony Ruprech to have the media screen raised for the next presentation. This next issue had been kept so secretive that Mark had discussed it only with Tony. It was now time to present it to the full board under strict confidence.

"When we announced our partnership for the alternate energy project and our intended public offering to raise funds to be used for development expenses and also as a substantial cash reserve for the company—money for a rainy day, as they say—I was contacted by the chairman of Globex Motors International currently the number four automaker in the world in terms of sales".

Mark took a sip of water and continued: "Globex was very interested in our strategy, impressed with our historical entrepreneurial spirit, and was particularly interested in entrenching its footprint in Canada. As a result, it made an offer to buy out our company, at par value". Looks of disbelief all around the table, Mark observed.

"Our stock price was at the time still depressed as a result of the recent regulatory and operational events, and so I rejected out-of-hand the offer that Globex presented. You don't sell out when you are down, especially if there's a plan for rehabilitation. Still, we agreed to keep in touch".

Tony sat down with a smile, as he inventoried the board members' body language. He saw confidence, trust and anxiety all merging in their facial expressions.

"As our stock began to increase in value and as we got closer to the full amount of capital we wanted to realize from the public offering, the increased stock price firmed up, volatility was reduced and volume became stabilized. It wasn't long, then, before Globex Motors made another offer. This is what Tony and I are here to present to you today".

The excitement in the conference room was palpable. Santius and its shareholders had suffered for many months. The company, once the darling of equity analysts, had later become a symbol of unplanned disarray and of individual corporate greed. This was great news, everyone felt, whatever the outcome, because it represented personal, professional and corporate redemption.

"Following a number of intensive discussions earlier this week, Globex has made a binding formal offer. The details are shown on the media screen", Mark motioned for the lights to be dimmed, "but essentially, Globex has offered us twenty-five million dollars to obtain an irrevocable option to buy up to forty-nine point nine percent of our shares within ninety days from today, at a premium of thirty-five percent over the average stock price during the last thirty days. Our shareholders will have the right to be paid out in cash or to convert their Santius shares to Globex Motors shares".

Mark stopped for a moment and as he made eye contact with every board member individually, he continued "this is an offer that Tony and I will be strongly recommending for acceptance. First, it provides twenty-five million dollars in cash. I will be shortly recommending how we can put that money to good use. Second, we will continue to have corporate control of Santius by having a majority of the outstanding shares, and we will have Santius representatives forming a majority of our board. Third, Santius will continue to be run as an autonomous public company and so we will see little change in our corporate environment, except of course, that we will have one of the world's biggest automakers as our permanent corporate partner. Moreover, our strategy partner and Santius will have a ready and profitable market in Globex Motors for the sale of our jointly-developed alternative energy project. This means that our future profits will come not only from the independent sale of Santius' own cars being powered by the new energy, but also from royalties earned from the sale of our technology to our partner Globex for use in its fleet of vehicles".

Mark stopped for a moment and then concluded: "And finally, our long-suffering shareholders will see an immediate jump in the value of their holdings if Globex exercises its option."

The excitement resulting from Mark's announcement overwhelmed him emotionally and, although he had negotiated every detail of the proposed agreement, Mark genuinely spoke as excitedly as if he were hearing the details for the very first time.

Before the board members had a chance to react, Mark concluded his presentation: "Now, as to how we spend the twenty-five million dollars from the Globex option . . .", Mark began ". . . our public offering will be very successful and we will have surplus cash reserves. We will not need to dip into the funds received from the Globex option for our ongoing operations or for any dividend payout to our shareholders."

Mark looked over his audience with satisfaction and announced: "Tony and I are recommending that we use the funds received from Globex to allocate five million dollars to a "Green Fund" to be used as a means to provide grants for environmental research on future projects to develop low emission energy. We believe it is important for our planet that we do this. Furthermore, it is an important corporate statement that perfectly defines our future corporate strategy". Mark noticed pride in the faces of all the board members, as they nodded their approval.

As to the remaining twenty million dollars, we recommend a one-time dividend distributed to all our shareholders of record as of the day we announce it. It is our way of thanking and rewarding our investors who have shown loyalty and commitment during the hard times and who have been patient with management and the board in rolling out the company's present and future plans.

"Finally, I want to thank my friend, our CEO Tony Ruprech. Tony was instrumental in every detail I presented today. We should all be very proud to have a leader with selfless qualities and with the skills that Tony has demonstrated".

Although Mark had wanted to spend as long as the board needed to discuss and debate Globex Motors' proposal, a board resolution approving the proposal was reached immediately. Everyone circled August 31 in their e-calendars as the date when Globex Motors' option was set to expire.

Mark sat down, emotionally exhausted. As everyone rose for a brief recess, Mark and Tony were surrounded by the others, congratulating them for their perseverance and for their creativity in having achieved so much in so little.

After the meeting and after the others had left, Tony approached Mark and thanked him for his congratulatory words. Tony was happy that, in Mark, he had a friend whose character was defined by generosity toward others, without any expectation of personal reward in return.

A simple but profound lesson Mark had learned from his aging grandfather many years earlier.

CHAPTER 59

At a meeting requested by Burton Cavendish's attorneys following the SEC's issuance of the dreaded "Wells Letter", Cavendish's two attorneys put on a brave face.

The same trio who had confronted Mark, now led by an even more confident legal zealot, would have none of it, however. With every comment made by Cavendish's attorneys, the legal beagle would simply respond "I'm sure Mr. Mark Gentile will attest otherwise" or "we believe Merkson will contradict that last statement" or "Mr. Tony Ruprech may well dispute your assertion".

After almost two hours consisting of a virtual monologue by Cavendish's representatives and repetitive staccato denials by the SEC's legal zealot, the Cavendish team asked for a recess to consider their client's deteriorating legal jeopardy.

"Burton, it's my obligation to give you advice in the face of the evidence the SEC has available", the more senior of his two attorneys said morosely, "it's clear that if we proceed to trial, your evidence will be contradicted by the senior executives of Santius, by the consultant

Merkson and by your former colleagues on the board. Mark Gentile will most likely drive the so-called last nail in your coffin. His evidence will have tremendous credibility with a jury because Gentile did the right thing—he resigned in the face of this crisis and he did so by abandoning a very substantial compensation package, choosing instead to stand by his personal ethical principles. This will have great traction with a jury who will likely find you guilty and, even worse, we will be facing an unsympathetic judge who will probably throw the proverbial "book" at you in sentencing".

The lawyer stopped for a moment and saw that his client had become a forlorn, isolated and defeated man. It was time for the punch-line, he thought: "I wouldn't be at all surprised if the judge wouldn't use your case as an example of what's rotten in our corporate system and sentence you to the maximum under his legal mandate."

After a brief pause, the attorney flipped through his notebook and added: "Frankly, Burton, we believe the jury will convict you and the judge will impose additive penalties of a very substantial fine and most likely a jail term. I know this is not what you want to hear, but we have an obligation to give you our honest opinion and assessment".

Burton Cavendish's color vanished from his face. He turned white as a ghost, and while he seemed to move his lips as if to say something, his voice was inaudible. *A disastrous way to end my career*, Cavendish thought.

"The timing of selling your options and stock portfolio was very unfortunate, Burton," his attorney continued, "You started selling the very day following your public statements to the shareholders indicating confidence in pursuing a strategic course that your CEO, Mark Gentile, your COO, Tony Ruprech, and the reputable consultant Merkson LLP all thought would lead to financial disaster". The weight of the evidence was now pushing Cavendish into a state of surrender. His lawyer, now sensing that he was close to receiving the instructions he wanted from his client, circled for the final kill: "You made over seventy-five million dollars in gains from your stock and options sales, all within a few weeks. Almost coincidentally with the sale of your last share, Santius' operations began to take a dive. This is devastating evidence we need to avoid being aired in a courtroom".

The legal instructions Cavendish's lawyers wanted to receive from their client was to negotiate a settlement and to avoid a trial at all costs. This result would be for the client's best interests, they correctly claimed. As well, these instructions would, at the same time, preserve the lawyers' interests because no lawyer wanted to be associated with a client's defeat at trial, especially a defeat as dramatic and complete as this was destined to become. Everything pointed to a resolution, they explained to their client with authority. With a confident and now unstoppable legal zealot on the other side of the table, all the cards seemed to be stacked against the former chairman of Santius.

The meeting ended that day without a settlement. The Cavendish team managed to obtain a brief standstill—a short period of time to allow them to consider more thoroughly the evidence the SEC had presented.

They all agreed to resume their discussions a week later. The SEC's parting words were that if no resolution to their satisfaction was reached within two weeks, the Agency would formally lay criminal charges and no further negotiations would be held.

The noose around Cavendish's neck drew tighter by several notches.

CHAPTER 60

One day before SEC's imposed deadline, a settlement was reached between Burton Cavendish and the SEC.

Under the terms of the consent order, Cavendish was to disgorge his entire seventy-five million dollars of profits from the Santius stock he had sold, pay a ten million dollar penalty for his wrongdoing and pay a further two million dollars for the SEC investigation expenses.

In addition, Burton Cavendish would be prohibited for life from serving in any public company as an officer, director or consultant. In exchange, the SEC agreed that it would not seek a jail term.

One month later, the Ontario Securities Commission, Canada's largest regulatory agency, issued its own charges modeled on the charges of the SEC.

Burton Cavendish settled the Canadian charges as well by agreeing to pay the OSC a fine of ten million dollars and the imposition of a similar life ban in Canada from holding office in any Canadian listed company.

Burton Cavendish's adventures in seeking to gain entry into the rarified circle of the ultra-privileged had come to a crashing and inglorious end.

CHAPTER 61

It was late August at Blue Mountain. The last vestiges of summer were now evident. The hills were exploding with wild flowers as Mark and Marina sat on the deck of their chalet. At the base of the mountain, three summer students were busy painting the chairlifts that, within three months, would be carrying excited skiers to the top of the "Happy Valley" ski trail.

The cicadas, though, seemed to pay little attention to Mark's thoughts about the oncoming ski season. Their chorus was shrill and continuous, interrupted now and then by some unexpected movements nearby but ready to resume their vocal celebration as soon as the impending danger had passed.

"An eventful few weeks", Mark whispered to Marina with a smile. "I couldn't have predicted half of the events that have occurred", replied Marina, "but Santius is now on the right path and everyone associated with the company feels good about what's happening . . . especially you, Mark. Dior and I are so proud of how you took on this role and handled yourself in carrying it out. You also should be proud of yourself".

Before Mark could reply, his cell phone rang. The otherwise familiar voice of Tony Ruprech was hardly recognizable through the excitement it carried: "Mark, I've been trying to reach you by email for half an hour. Is this one of those rare times you actually logged off?", Tony asked incredulously. "I'm a part-timer now, Tony", Mark said with a chuckle.

Mark quickly logged on, and on his screen appeared the following letter:

August 22, 2012

NOTICE

Globex Motors International hereby gives you notice that it proposes to exercise its option to acquire the optioned shares pursuant to the terms of the Option Agreement, effective August 31, 2012.

J. S. Thornton
CEO and Chairman
Globex Motors International

Three days later, Mark Gentile and the CEO and Chairman of Globex met to discuss the underlying details of the partial acquisition.

The terms of the corporate affiliation were quickly agreed upon and included the decision that Santius would be operated as a wholly autonomous company; that Tony Ruprech would be offered a long term contract to be its CEO; and that, for a minimum of three years, Mark Gentile would serve in the dual role of board member of Globex and as Chairman of Santius.

Although Mark and Tony had been given the board's full authorization to implement the deal with Globex in the event Globex exercised its option, nevertheless, in the interest of a fully participatory decision-making process, Mark brought the proposed agreement back to the board for ratification. Expectedly, the agreement was accepted unanimously and without discussion.

Following the Santius board meeting at which the agreement was unanimously ratified, Mark and Tony congratulated each other. "We did it, Tony. We did it", Mark whispered almost whimsically.

"No, *you* did it, Mark. You did it. This was your project from beginning to end. Thank you for taking me along for the ride", replied his friend, emotionally.

Mark left the Santius building, headed for his car. He dialled his home number and told Marina the good news. "Round up Dior and meet me at Fabrizio's for dinner in an hour. There's much to celebrate".

Mark sat back in his car, opened the window and inhaled deeply. There was a hint of crispness in the air. His mind was flashing back to the accumulated memories of the last year. His thoughts were racing, as if each fleeting thought was trying to get to the finish line first, but constantly tripping over one another.

Mark turned on the engine and then immediately turned it off. He concluded that, in his current state of inebriating euphoria, he was unfit to drive. He dialled for a taxi and waited for its arrival, alone but content.

CHAPTER 62

After two intensive weeks of fraternizing with Santius' lawyers, accountants and bankers, all the legal and financial details were resolved in a comprehensive agreement with Globex that was now ready for final approval. As process dictated, the agreement required the approval by the executive teams of both companies and, thereafter, by the boards of both Santius and Globex.

It was exactly three months since Mark's return from Italy that had started Santius' financial and legal workout. Mark could perhaps be forgiven for being somewhat sentimental as he called to order the last board meeting of Santius as a stand-alone company.

Nevertheless, Mark mused silently, *while Globex had become an important minority partner in Santius, its operational independence had been retained. Santius would continue to operate as it always had, in the same philosophical and entrepreneurial spirit of its founder, Gordon Welsh.*

Going forward, this was going to be a more aggressive and confident Santius, knowing that its corpulent partner lay in the background silently, providing to Santius its wisdom and experience, as needed. Mark, as the continuing chairman of Santius and as a board member of Globex, was the chosen "bridge" for carrying information from one company to the other.

"My friends", Mark began once the chatter of excitement had abated, "this is indeed a day that all of us will remember as the turning point in Santius' corporate life. We have graduated to the next level and I have all of you to thank for your hard work and cooperation, especially over the last few weeks. The agreement we will sign today is your reward for the difficult times you have endured. Thank you for asking me to be a part of this experience". With these simple words, Mark sat down and motioned to the corporate secretary to hand out several copies of the final document to Tony first, for signature. Mark's signature would make the agreement final.

The corporate secretary swung around the table and dutifully placed in front of Tony one copy after the next for him to sign. He collected the signed copies and headed toward Mark at the head of the table for his final signature. As Mark lifted his pen, the rest of the board rose as one and applauded loudly while Mark began to sign the papers.

Mark's eyes were moist with emotion. He felt as if a weight had been lifted off his shoulders, as if he had finally vanquished his stubborn internal demons.

PART 4

CHAPTER 63

On this warm late September day, the lazy waters of the Bradano River meandered slowly in the floor of the surrounding hills. The river divided several mountain ranges, each of which was spiked with hilltop towns. On each such hilltop lay a small, proud village, among them Acerenza, Mark's beloved hometown. Each such town had been founded two thousand years earlier at the time when the Saracens, Longobards and Greeks battled for the area's dominance.

The scorching summer heat had not yet abated in this part of the world. The Bradano River had been reduced to a trickle flowing gently, imperceptibly, in this direction and that while accommodating the existing contours of the topography it encountered along its pre-destined path. A quick rush of the waters over a protruding rock or tree branch would detour the flow temporarily, only to be again reconnected in a seemingly directionless, and yet defined, destination toward the Ionian Sea.

Mark sat on a large rock in his vineyard, sloping downward toward the valley, all the while mesmerized by the lazy waters as they desperately sought to re-energize themselves along their journey.

The mellow late afternoon sun, still warm in its embrace, soothed Mark's spirits. This had been an intensive, but very satisfying, few months, Mark concluded. Much had been accomplished in a short period of time. He felt a sense of pride in having taken part in salvaging Santius from certain doom. He felt optimistic that this company had again assumed a sense of purpose. Its corporate and financial future was assured. He felt excited by the new roles he would be playing in rolling out its newly-adopted strategies.

At times, after his resignation from Santius a year and a half earlier, Mark had felt insecure in his decision to leave the company at that moment of crisis. At other times, he had convinced himself that he had no other choice but to resign as he did so to avoid an internal battle that would pit the company's management against its board of directors—a battle in which there would be no winners and only one loser: Santius.

Mark pondered over the tumultuous events of the last year, all the while allowing his eyes to inspect Alvanello's vineyards and olive groves. As far as his eyes could see, rows upon rows of vines with their dangling fruits: aglianico and moscato grapes each absorbing the last rays of the sun before being harvested for the annual rite of "*La Vendemmia*"—the grape harvest.

"It will be a very fine Vendemmia", a familiar voice from behind announced with pride. "Santiana—Vino will have an excellent year of wine production". Luca Moranni sat next to Mark, his hand on Mark's shoulder. Luca knew exactly where to find his friend on a warm, sunny afternoon. With a small satchel of homemade cheese, freshly-baked *focaccia* and a bottle of Santiana's own fine *Aglianico,* Luca knew that he would find his friend in the Alvanello vineyard, among his vines.

"*Ben tornato*"—welcome back—Marco", Luca said as the two old friends smiled and hugged each other. "I heard from Marina in town that you had quite an exciting few months back in Toronto", Luca continued with a smile. "But now you are back here and we have hard work to do . . .", and with a wink and a smile, ". . . and life to enjoy. So, no more worries and no more looking back", Luca now-turned—bon-vivant ordered emphatically.

Mark and Luca enjoyed the afternoon eating cheese and *focaccia* and drinking wine. "How can we toast our good health and our friendship without glasses?" Mark poked fun at this friend. Luca at once sprung to his feet, ambled down to the first row of vines, inspected them carefully and then tore away two large vine leaves. He sat down and expertly folded them individually until he created two cups. He handed one to his friend and filled it with wine. He then filled his own and, with a benign smile, Luca raised his wine cup: "Not one drop of wine wasted! This is why the grape and the vine are so important to our way of life in this part of Italy", Luca the philosopher—king pontificated, "the vine is a vessel through its leaves; a spiritual and nutritious nourishment through its wine, a fruit through its grapes and Christ's very blood in its liquid form. It is the essence of life itself", he concluded triumphantly, without fear of contradiction. Indeed, not a drop of the precious liquid was spilled in the process.

The two friends toasted to their friendship, to their loved ones, to their good fortune and to life itself.

Mark and Luca, two close friends during the first half dozen years of their lives in the small town of Acerenza, had each chosen a different path, a world apart. Perhaps it was pre-determined destiny that had brought them together again many decades later, to resume their interrupted friendship. Mark concluded that it was best to leave these intriguing mysteries of life unscrambled, without seeking out answers or explanations.

There, sitting on a rock in the middle of Alvanello's vineyards, with nature serving as their conference room, without a pre-scheduled meeting and without a fixed agenda, the two friends-turned business partners, began to discuss the operational details of the imminent Vendemmia.

When the last of the day's rays began to retreat behind the mountain set to abandon them for the night, Mark and Luca rose and after one final peak at nature's theatre around them, the two friends set out for their return to town.

CHAPTER 64

After a few days in Acerenza, Mark and Marina settled back to the slower pace of their daily activities.

For Mark, in comparison to the frenetic life back in Santius' offices during the last few months, the pace in Acerenza was glacial. But not for the Acerenzesi. The Vendemmia season was as busy as life became in this idyllic town. One could feel the vibes of expectancy in the air. The citizenry was excited. This, after all, was the time when they would be seeking nature's rewards for their continuous efforts that had begun in late February. Like the Acerenzesi children waiting for La Befana to make its annual January ruling on their behavior during the previous year in order to dole out their corresponding just rewards, the adult Acerenzesi anxiously undertook their final preparations for the results of the Vendemmia.

But, while the final score would be postponed until all the results were in, the Acerenzesi were no fools. Their effervescence unmasked their jubilation over the expected success of this year's Vendemmia. The weather had been perfect, just enough moisture for growth and plenty of sunshine toward late summer. Crisp September nights and bright autumn days. A perfect merger of the necessary weather phenomena to ensure a bountiful "*raccolta*"—harvest—of the Aglianico grapes.

No one was more excited than Mark's partner, Luca Moranni. "This will be the best Vendemmia in recent memory", gushed Luca, as he devoured a "*cornetto al cioccolato*", at Budini's Caffé. "Very little spoilage, he continued, "the grapes are plump and juicy. We expect not just quality but also quantity".

Mark listened to Luca's enthusiasm with pride. Luca's transformation from the self-anointed and unaided police chief to senior executive and partner of the Santiana group of companies was now complete. In fact, Mark had marvelled at how Luca's "*dolce far niente*" past lifestyle had now become for him a frenzied, new world of budgets, *pro formas*, earnings and market capitalizations for each of the Santiana subsidiaries and, on a consolidated basis, for the controlling holding company, Santiana International. Remarkably, though, Luca seemed to have retained and enviable balance between ambition and an easy life-style for which Italians, and particularly Southern Italians, are known. It seemed that Luca had learned the secret of seamlessness on how to be "Mr. Moranni" while discharging his business functions and the boisterous, generous and happy-go-lucky "Luca" seamlessly, when mingling among the almost three thousand full-time residents of the town.

Over a second espresso, the two friends continued to discuss general plans for their newly-created food and winery empire. "Maybe it's time for us to start thinking about taking Santius International—how you say it—'public' on the *Borsa*—the stock market? That would give us more opportunity, no?" Luca suggested inquisitively but with sufficient confidence in his voice to show Mark that he had done some research on the topic.

Somewhat surprised by Luca's comment, but not totally shocked by it given the huge strides he had made in his development from lone cop to business executive, Mark smiled at his friend and replied "Maybe later,

Luca. Right now we still have a lot of work to do before we get to that point, my friend, and I'll need your help to get it done".

Temporarily satisfied with his answer, Luca and Mark walked toward "*il Fossato*"—the piazza where Luca had installed the new headquarters of Santiana International.

CHAPTER 65

Over the next days, Santiana's offices were a hub of activity. There was a constant flow of employees parading in and out, as the ramp-up to the start of the grape harvest began.

The operational group, led by Luca, was busy lining up the various contractors for the harvesting of the grapes and their eventual transformation into liquid gold. A far cry, Mark thought, from his heady days as a six-year old when he, Marco, and his grandfather would crush the grapes under foot within the large cement basin in their cantina.

Almost six decades later, Mark's Santiana was now permanently employing over one hundred diligent employees and many others seasonally, owned its own warehouse, produced its own branded Santiana-Vino for export to over a dozen countries through Santiana's well-defined marketing and distribution networks.

Mark watched the continuous procession of bodies in and out of the various offices in Santiana's headquarters, with satisfaction and personal pride at what had been accomplished in such a short time. He felt a sense of accomplishment in the knowledge that his recently-founded business not only put Acerenza on the map, but had also instilled in each of its residents a sense of personal pride.

Indeed, a quiet transformation had taken place within the last eighteen months. The "*Made in Acerenza*" on the thousands of bottles of Aglianico sold in different parts of the globe had converted sleepy and isolated Acerenza to a center where important business was now being transacted at Santiana, where business types in suits and with briefcases, mingled in cafés seamlessly with farmers and retailers. So much so, that Mark's next project would involve the construction of a hotel-restaurant in the centre of the ancient town so as to accommodate not only the sizeable Santiana clientele but also the increased number of tourists who made a special effort to visit the little town that produced that very pleasant Santiana-Vino. An important side-benefit from these Santiana-driven activities was the revitalization of the historic center of the "old town" on the hilltop—an unexpected reversal from the previously abandoned ancient homes in favor of the newer "*villette*" outside the gates of San Canio, where more abundant land availability and more progressive construction processes had attracted the younger generation of Acerenzesi to create the first, and only, suburb of Acerenza. But now, the old center was buzzing as the residents began to repatriate their once-abandoned homes.

Mainly as a result of the successes of Santiana-Vino and Santiana-Alimentari, the Acerenza town council, for the first time in its history, had created a tourist marketing board, trumpeting the town's laid-back "*dolce vita*" as a respite from the stresses of modern life. While a far cry from experiencing the hordes of tourists of Venice, Florence or Rome, nevertheless, it was no longer unusual to find Germans, English or North American tourists, cameras strapped on their shoulders, visiting the Cathedral and meandering through the cobblestoned streets where the only form of transportation for centuries had been, and would likely always be, one's own two feet or atop protesting donkeys and mules.

Mark's reflections were suddenly broken by Luca's tap on his shoulder announcing: "Mark, the clock has struck noon. It's time for us to get ready to eat. I do all the work around here and you do all the thinking, *amico mio*—my friend. We make a fine pair, you and me. We may have to renegotiate an increase in my ownership in Santiana", Luca suggested with a wink.

Over lunch, Mark suggested to Luca that, in this age of new technology, it was perhaps now appropriate to roll back time and recommence the now-lost tradition of grape-stomping.

"What do you say, Luca, about having Santiana sponsor a week-long festival during the Vendemmia season?" Mark began to unfold his idea. "The celebration would include a promotion of our locally-produced wines and foods. A central focus of the festival would include a contest that would have pairs consisting of fathers and grandfathers with their children and grandchildren reviving the lost art of crushing grapes the traditional way, with one's own feet. We could dream up a competition and award to the winners a prize including a bountiful variety of all of Santiana's products", Luca added Luca enthusiastically. "We could have a wine and local foods event and we could invite the media to cover the grape festival and make the Vendemmia activities become an annual tradition that could also attract tourists to our town", he concluded triumphantly. And so, ideas kept coming, each different, each intended to put a brand on Acerenza and its glorious history.

While these ideas needed to be further developed, Mark desperately sought a new way to keep alive the personal experiences he had enjoyed with his grandfather, experiences that youthful Marco had so much cherished and that he had now stored as memories forever locked in his heart.

CHAPTER 66

By the end of November, activities in Acerenza were winding down. With the busy and successful Vendemmia season behind them and the olives now crushed and distilled into pure extra-virgin olive oil. The locals were now getting ready for the seasonal lull that would be interrupted only by the Santa Lucia celebrations on December 13 and, immediately thereafter, the beginning of the Christmas festivities that would begin in mid-December and end at the Epiphany in early January.

Until late February, the unofficial arrival of spring, the good citizens of Acerenza took the time to stop, reenergize and reacquaint themselves with friends and family following the continuous frenetic pace of the previous nine months. During this period of rest and reflection, the cafés became their temples where they convened to brag, argue, play cards, discuss politics and, of course, debate their passion, *calcio*—soccer.

This was the time when every olive-picker and grape-crusher magically reached new levels of oratory excellence and political acumen. When every farmer became an instant manager or coach of his favorite soccer team, disputing this team line-up and that decision to trade or acquire a player. Many just spent time gossiping about nothing, much like a *Seinfeld* episode: a hundred "George Costanza's" would passionately plead a subject of little or no importance but with a personal passion that made it life or death. Form became substance during these dialogues. Form became meaningful. Form became the enviable art of creating a theme, moulding it into an oratorical cadence, coding it with eloquence and then using pure talent to elevate it into a subject that would be passionately debated for hours, detouring now and again into uncharted tributaries, spawning simultaneously in several directions but with no end and no conclusions.

The only substantive beneficiaries of this repeated spectacle were the café owners who were required to provide a continuous flow of libation and nourishment to the assembled spectators and to the main combatants themselves.

This environment, in its contradiction of passive activity, this theatre of energy-laden philosophers, was the perfect forum for Mark Gentile to think about the recent corporate activities back in Toronto, and to reflect on whether he could give his personal contribution a passing grade.

Acerenza, in the quiet off-season, was perhaps the only appropriate place where Mark could reflect on his cauldron of bubbling emotions and determine whether he could now finally find that elusive peace in his soul that had been so difficult for him to obtain.

A cool wind swooped down across the lower Apennines late one evening as Mark and Marina, hand in hand, walked briskly home after a dinner out with friends. "It's beginning to feel like it will be a colder winter than usual", Marina whispered as they hurried their pace toward the Acerenza Municipal Office, a few blocks away from their home. "We've had a great Vendemmia this year", replied Mark. "The season is now changing. It's time for us all to replenish our minds and our spirits. The cycle of life renews itself, each part a necessary component of the others. Nature, with its unshakeable forces, is our orchestra leader, paving the way for our actions . . ."

Without skipping a beat, Marina replied "and this lowly member of the orchestra is telling you that we should hasten our pace. This cold wind is penetrating right through my body", she replied matter-of-factly, putting an end, at least temporarily, to perhaps the start of yet another philosophical introspection by her husband.

CHAPTER 67

Even in the month of February, when the northern parts of North America are enveloped by cold and darkness, southern Italians bravely sit at outdoor cafés, armed with a cigarette in one hand and a warm cappuccino in the other, surveying the landscape of people, dogs, storekeepers and customers playing out their daily lives. And so it is also in the village of Positano, frenetic in the summer and autumn but now sleepy in its invernal hibernation.

Aided, at times, by gas-fuelled heating lamps, they will linger for hours supposedly reading the latest *Gazzetta Dello Sport* but, in reality, one eye scanning the latest soccer results while the other busily searching for a human target with whom to exchange "*due chiacchiere*"—a few words—on the latest daily scandal impacting their beloved Peninsula.

It is part of what Italians are: a people who, by their very nature, are passionate and effervescent, involved and extroverted. A normal conversation between two participants will, by its tone, volume and passion of delivery, invariably be misinterpreted by a foreigner as a serious relationship rupture. In reality, however, these protagonists are merely expressing their innermost feelings with a bravado and a force that can be understandably mistaken as warring controversy. On and on they go at full tilt with their oratory, never giving an inch, always committed to taking no prisoner.

At some point in the debate, they stop almost on cue, and one or the other motions the server to bring more refreshments. Re-energized, they now resume their verbal jousting until they decide to declare a draw. It's important that there be no loser in such battle of words. Each recognizes that "*fare la brutta figura*"—being shamed—needs to be avoided at all costs. How else than by a scoreless draw, can these modern-day warriors participate in a future debate, on the same or some other subject, later in this, or on another day?

Back in their villletta on the Amalfi coast, after Mark's solitary early morning run, the couple's daily morning routine for Mark and Marina invariably started with a walk down from their home slowly along the narrow streets of Positano, large canvass bag in hand, examining which of the small grocery stores displayed the freshest fruits and vegetables for their daily needs. At least once a week, they would continue their journey to their favorite seafood store right on the water's edge, waiting for the latest catch of the day to come in, more or less, at a predetermined time. The type of seafood caught was usually of secondary importance. The key was that it be freshly caught. Marina would always insist that she personally examine the "catch" and then bargain with the fishermen over price. "*Signora Gentile*", one or the other of the fishermen could be heard saying, while all the time smiling benevolently, "*con clienti come lei, come facciamo a vivere noi altri?*"—with customers like you, how can we make a living?

There would then follow brief exchanges about the respective families' health, firm handshakes all around, with mutual promises to meet again, same place same time, later this week or early the next.

With a sense of contentment permeating their being, the two long-time mates, clasping each other's free hand, would then head toward Nunzio's Caffé for their mid-morning cappuccino, before starting up the Scalinata to their home at the top.

CHAPTER 68

For Mark, this particular winter in Positano was a time for self-analysis. He had accomplished much this past year. He had righted what he came to believe were his previous omissions. Mark had gone back into the lion's den and had largely succeeded in resuscitating a moribund Santius from certain passing. In so doing, he had rebuilt his own dignity and had reenergized his personal moral fibre.

Mark had lived most of the last two years in a state of contradiction: hero and villain, victor and vanquished, with moral achievement and in shameful abandonment. *Who is the real Mark Gentile?* he asked himself. At times, he fully understood himself; at other times, he felt as if part of him was a stranger.

"Often, in the months following my resignation from Santius, I have felt like I didn't know myself, like I had a split personality", Mark would often confide in Marina, "I felt my being was shaped in two distinct persons, with one not fully understanding the other . . .". Sensing her husband's pain in retelling his innermost feelings, Marina would comfort Mark gently and lovingly "It's understandable, my love", she would whisper, "you have gone through a lot of personal turmoil, with conflicting emotions trying to determine right from wrong", Marina would conclude, hoping that her comforting words would help her husband reach finality.

But Mark's personal turmoil had been so ingrained as to almost become innate. He often compared his own state of mind to that of his favorite poet, Petrarca, who often mused that his love, Laura, was an emblematic being whom he didn't always understand: one day, Laura was her normal self; the next, she became unrecognizable. Like Petrarca, Mark felt that he hadn't firmly staked out his true character, that he had merely fluctuated in contradiction, without clarity and without finality.

Mark had failed to clarify his own identity, perhaps because he hadn't fully appreciated neither the gravity not the repercussions of Burton Cavendish's self-centred objectives. Perhaps, he had often feared, because he hadn't had the courage to clearly and firmly separate himself from the very objectives he condemned.

And so, Mark had lived in purgatory, in a state of contradiction: he wanted to run as far as he could from Cavendish's immorality, and yet felt the need to return to it and set it right. He had distanced himself from the epicentre of his turmoil and yet he had longed to return to it. He wanted to escape, both physically and mentally into activities that would make him forget, and yet he wanted to remember. At times, he slipped into a melancholy state that would be all-consuming, until that distant whisper summoned him and compelled him to use all his inner strength to heed its call.

The last few months had served not only to allow Mark to resurrect Santius but also to defeat the unethical and immoral self-centredness that, in Mark's mind, Burton Cavendish represented. In the end, Mark felt exhilarated, euphoric, satisfied that he had filled his void. He felt a vindication not so much for himself but more for the ethics that, he knew, should be the underpinnings of every person's life.

Mark Gentile had escaped, returned and confronted his personal demons. He had succeeded in finally quelling their conspiracy to derail the internal stability of his emotions. As a result, he had become a stronger and more confident person. Someone who had touched bottom and who had bounced up again. Someone who was rising from the depths of despair to some semblance of normalcy.

CHAPTER 69

Santius and its parent, Globex Motors International, each had monthly telephonic board meetings to review the more substantial operational and financial issues that the management of each company undertook on a daily basis. Each company had scheduled quarterly board meetings on the first Tuesday of every fourth month. Every member's personal attendance was mandatory at the quarterly meetings because it was at these meetings where there would be a full review of the previous quarter's financial, legal and operational activities. Most importantly, the quarterly meetings also included a full discussion of strategic issues and plans for the future.

As chairman of Santius, it was Mark's responsibility not only to lead the Santius board into these reviews and discussions but also, in his dual capacity as Globex board member, to be the pipeline to Globex of all such discussions and decisions in order to ensure that they were consistent with, and therefore fit within, Globex's overall strategic plan.

Mark's initial fear that Globex, as Santius' legal parent, might subtly impose its influence on Santius' decisions proved to be unfounded.

Globex allowed Santius to operate autonomously and, in fact, was very supportive of the creative ideas flowing up from its affiliate. Santius' management was in the enviable position of running its own company without interference while, at the same time, having its muscled partner back all its financial needs.

In this almost idyllic corporate environment, Santius began its remarkable recovery in short order. Under Tony Ruprech's operational leadership and Mark's strategic guidance, Santius' once-creative energies once again flowed freely. In turn, this newly-recaptured entrepreneurial spirit was reflected in a higher morale within the organization. Once again, Santius' employees were proud of the company they served. The best and most creative minds in the automotive industry applied for employment with Santius, eager to become part of this renewed success story.

At times, reputations can take decades to earn and minutes to be destroyed. With hard work and perseverance, Santius had demonstrated that the downward spiral could quickly be reversed if indeed the newly-created energies are sincere and are based on an unshakeable commitment to succeed. Everyone wanted to be part of a success story, and Santius was once again a success story.

Gordon Welsh, the founder and CEO of Santius, the person who had single-handedly chosen Mark to be his successor and who had instilled in young Mark the principles of ethics and integrity that governed his own life and, later, Mark's life, would have been proud of what Santius had become, Mark thought with a smile of contentment.

With these experiences behind him, Mark was more determined than ever to ensure that those principles of honesty, integrity and fair-dealing would be the tenets that, in the future, would continue to guide both his professional and his personal life.

CHAPTER 70

By mid-April, Mark was back at the Santius offices in Toronto in his new permanent role as chairman of the board. A palpable transformation had occurred at Santius since the clearing of the company's overhanging clouds. Activities could be seen everywhere; a new sense of purpose was evident both with executives in the management offices and with the "rank and file" in the corridors. A sense of optimism seemed to pervade the company and engulfed everyone. Employees were once again proud to be associated with Santius in the knowledge, and with the commitment, that this company was now destined to be a significant contributor to, and make a positive difference, in the world of alternate energy and, as a result, in the world we would be leaving behind to our children.

Perhaps most symbolic of the newly-rediscovered optimism for the present day and for the future, the digital board that provided an instant play-by-play of Santius' stock performance had been reinstalled in the lobby, where it had stood during Mark's tenure as CEO. There, employees would often stop for a second to peek at the live numbers on the screen confirming Santius' stock performance, and, thereby, Santius' corporate report card.

Mark met privately with his long-time colleague and friend Tony Ruprech to discuss all the key issues for the upcoming board meeting. "I can't recall ever having had a meeting like this with your predecessor before any of our board meetings", Tony said, avoiding uttering the name Burton Cavendish, choosing the more neutral description "your predecessor" instead.

Tony explained that the process with Mark's "predecessor" had been simple: Cavendish drafted the agenda; he distributed it; he took the lead in presenting those issues he wished to table; and then asked me or one of the other managers present to fill in the details, as needed. It was autocracy at its worst".

Tony stopped for emphasis, and then continued ". . . and yet, he worked extremely hard to create an illusion of full, participatory democracy. Looking at it now, it was quite farcical. But nobody objected. Noone did anything about it."

"What about discussion of the issues"? Mark asked.

"He answered all questions and when he couldn't personally do it, he would usually ask me to answer the question as reformulated by him so as to solicit from me the answer he sought. The meetings were illusory and superfluous. The resolutions passed had always been pre-determined".

Tony sat in silence for a long minute, no doubt reflecting on what he had said, realizing that his accusations were as much an indictment on the orchestra leader as they were on the entire orchestra, including him, for blindly following the lead of a straying conductor.

"Well, Tony, we don't need to spend too much more time worrying about the past. The company and our shareholders have now entrusted us to carve out the future, to implement a strategic plan they have approved. We have an important job to do; corporate, financial and operational objectives to fulfill".

With Mark's last comment as a guide, they developed their board presentation with Mark's insistence that Tony should be the presenter.

Mark gently dismissed Tony's protestations and added "I'm like the coach of a soccer team. I direct, I guide, I even decide who plays and who sits on the bench. But I don't actually get on the pitch. I don't score goals and I don't stop the ball from going into the net".

"But tell me, Mark, that as coach you will also be dressed to play and can step on the field the moment you're needed . . ." offered Tony inquisitively, continuing with Mark's metaphor.

"In full playing gear and, playing or coaching, I'm always with my game-face on", Mark answered with determination, and a smile.

Tony saw a dramatic change in his friend's style from his earlier executive days during Cavendish's chairmanship. He was now much more participatory, much more willing to give credit to the other members of the team.

"Promise me, Mark" Tony asked as he placed his hand benignly around Mark's shoulder, "if you intend to use the team metaphor again with others and want to have maximum impact, remember that you are now back in Canada where hockey and not soccer is considered 'the beautiful game'".

CHAPTER 71

It had been an unusually warm summer in Toronto with temperatures that while they didn't quite rival those of southern Italy, nonetheless, with the high humidity as a factor, the days were hot and the evenings languid.

Mark and Marina had passed a glorious few months in Toronto relaxing, eating "*al fresco*", and generally catching up on social activities with friends and family that had been interrupted, or postponed, by Mark's busy schedule the previous year.

Dior had been progressing steadily in her employment with the consulting firm Merkson LLC and had recently been promoted associate vice-president, the youngest in that Firm's storied history—"one of two dozen AVP's . . ." Dior had modestly explained to her dad when he offered her his congratulations.

". . . besides, I'm only there temporarily to get some experience so that I can help you with the Santiana food and wine empire", she enquired smilingly but with a firmness that delighted Mark.

And so it went with Mark and Marina these past few weeks, enjoying the life they had left behind. Before too long, they found themselves totally re-immersed with their normal daily activities.

The warmth of July and August had, however, largely retreated by the middle of September, consistently with predictable Canadian weather patterns. At their Blue Mountain chalet, one could particularly feel the briskness in the air. Even the cicadas, always hiding furtively in the tall hillside grass and wildflowers, screamed out their *cantata's* somewhat apprehensively, no doubt sensing the onset of the colder weather.

Early one September evening, armed with a double dose of strong espresso, Mark sat on his back deck facing the mountain, his mind relaxed but alert and in a contemplative mood. It seemed to Mark that this was the perfect ambiance within which to review the immediate past and consider their future plans.

At that moment, however, a seagull circled half-way up the slope, soon joined by several others. The flock's future plans and their itinerary were also being drawn up to deal with the imminent change of seasons.

CHAPTER 72

Mark drew a long sip from his coffee cup and thought about his life to that point. It had been a long, and at times, arduous journey, he thought. His mind raced back to more than half a century of accumulated memories. Half a century of upbringing in North America: his education, his experiences growing up, his provocative college and law school days that had shaped his cultural and spiritual framework, the law firm he had joined, the senior executive roles he had enjoyed. He thought affectionately about his wonderful marriage to Marina who had become his soul-mate and best friend, the birth of his daughter Dior and the experience of seeing her grow from a toddler to the amazing person she had become, his friends, his colleagues, the cafés he had frequented in Toronto that had served for him a refuge for his internal reflections.

Mark stopped the movie reel to admire the beauty of his surroundings. He now had the time to gaze without hurry, or to close his eyes and visualize with his mind what lay beyond the mountain.

In brief, Mark felt that his past way of life had formed a formidable and irresistible magnet pulling him back to his adopted homeland. But not totally, and certainly not exclusively. Mark had worked hard for his financial and societal successes in North America, and for his way of life. He concluded that it would not be possible for him to give them up. Nor did he wish to do so, for they had become part of who he was, who he had become.

And yet, the works of the Italian greats had also ingrained in his soul that sense of Italian culture that, by now, had become an indelible part of who Mark was. Since his rebellious university days, he had devoured the poetry of Petrarca and the symbolism of Dante's *Divine Comedy.* He had found humor and fascination with Boccaccio's erotic tales. He had been provoked by Luigi Pirandello's deep philosophy represented by the seemingly simple refrain of "*Cosi e' se vi pare-It is so, if you believe it to be so*". He had been affected by the subtle and descriptive meanings in the romantic novels of Italian literature. Mark had also been greatly influenced by the great Renaissance philosophers. He had, at first, been impressed and provoked by the harsh realities of the principles pronounced in Nicolo' Macchiavelli's "The Prince". Later, however, as maturity set in and as the twin *formulae* of ethics and morality began to invade his being, he had learned to distance himself from the notion that the end always justified the means of achieving it. *Surely,* Mark eventually concluded, *if the means leads to an immoral or unethical or criminal end, such end can't ever be said to justify the means of achieving it.*

And while Mark could not appreciate art, music and science to the same extent as literature, philosophy and poetry, still he enjoyed these other forms of expression and felt proud that he had been born in a country that had given so much to the world; that, single-handedly, had taken Europe and the known world by the hand and had carried it through the *Rinascimento*—the Rennaisance, the global reawakening that had changed the world forever, and that had changed it for the better.

Two forces of formidable strengths, each with characteristics so intrinsically intertwined in Mark that a division of these forces, or a choosing of one over the other, he felt, would leave a chasm, a void, in his soul that would be incapable of being repaired.

Mark's reverie was interrupted by Marina's arrival with a cup of tea in hand. "I was just thinking of the wonderful life we have enjoyed . . .", Mark greeted his wife with a kiss.

Sensing that Mark was in a contemplative mood, Marina said simply: "Yes, we are so fortunate to be able to share as a family, and with our friends, the ability to bridge these two wonderful and quite different worlds and cultures, and blend them into one". Marina's voice trailed off. She kissed her husband lovingly.

Mark smiled his approval. "Yes, we are fortunate", he replied softly, his eyes moist with emotion.

CHAPTER 73

In the distance, breaking the quietude of the mountain, a group of young men could be heard singing a vaguely familiar Justin Bieber hip-hop tune. They were busy singing, talking, laughing—but with scrapers and paint brushes in hand, they were also busy at work in a sort of human chain. First the scrapers, attacking the peeling blue paint from the exterior of the dismounted ski lifts sitting in neat rows on the hillside, and then the painters restoring their faded lustre with shiny blue paint.

Mark and Marina lingered over their drinks for a long time, holding hands and watching, with amusement, the paint restoration project. "They're getting the lifts and the trails ready for the ski season", offered Marina. And as for us, Mr. Gentile, we also have a busy few days ahead of us getting ready to return to Acerenza for the start of the grape harvest season. After all, Santiana-Vino needs you once again to wave your magic wand so that it will have another successful year".

"Skis are like suit ties." Mark smiled, "One year they're short and wide; the next, long and narrow. My skis are out of date. Time to visit

Red Devil Sports in the Village for a new set that will patiently wait for our return here after the Vendemmia in Acerenza".

Marina lodged her head on Mark's chest and softly began humming the Bieber tune in unison with the boys on the hill-side.

Mark smiled. He placed his arm over Marina's shoulder and pulled her tightly to him.

"It's going to be a clear evening" whispered Mark. "Nature will soon be putting on her black dress with sparkles . . .", his voice lost in the emptiness of the mountain.

There, the two soul-mates remained in a gentle embrace, witnesses to the sun setting behind the slopes.

Mark's body was motionless, totally relaxed. His mind had finally found peace.

EPILOGUE

Two points on a map, separated by Poseidon's domain. Diverse, yet similar, distinct yet joined in Siamese union. Each representing a culture and a people fiercely proud and independent, living in a global society that tends toward global assimilation but, at the same time, strives to provide a life for its citizenry characterized by the uniqueness of its own distinct customs.

And, in this way, the idyllic town of Acerenza, sitting proudly and permanently atop a far-away mountain in an isolated region of Southern Italy continues to contribute to certain essential life principles long since forgotten, or conveniently set aside, within a frenetic global community.

This same setting had provided to Mark Gentile the perfect forum for him to embark on his internal spiritual odyssey. Its gentle environment, virtually unchanged through the centuries, had allowed for gradual and unforced reflection. Through the physical beauty of its surroundings, the charm and generosity of its people and the childhood memories experienced half a century earlier, Mark-turned-Marco Gentile had filled the void in his soul with some of life's most treasured underpinnings:

finding a balance between innate ambition and generosity of spirit; between the need to succeed and the necessity of doing so ethically; understanding the importance not only of following the laws of man predicated by codified rules but also, and importantly, of abiding by the unwritten and subjective rules of conduct that allow for harmonious and ethical co-existence.

Half a century later, Mark Gentile reconfirmed in his own mind his grandfather's simple teachings. Indeed, Mark came to understand, adopt and implement his grandfather's oft-repeated lessons that to be truly happy, one must learn to act without the expectation of any external reward; that one must engage in an activity simply because it is the right thing to do; that the inner satisfaction of having engaged in fair dealing is ultimately the only just reward that matters—an ethereal reward, to be sure, but one that leads to inner fulfillment.

These simple but powerful principles, transferred by an aging grandfather to a receptive grandson many years earlier in a small and isolated hilltop town, if followed, would dramatically alter our daily lives. And alter them for the better.

APPENDIX

Although it's been over ten years since the passing of my mother-in-law, Francesca, I can still hear her voice: "come Anita, today we make a new dish from my mother in the old country".

Memories inevitably fade away with the passage of time, and I am quite certain that many of the "secrets" I inherited from Francesca have stayed with her. Nevertheless, the amalgamated smells of those wonderful concoctions will always remain with me: the smells of the various spices she would expertly mix in her sauces and marinades; the convalescence of oregano, basil, garlic and *peperoncino* she added to her *ragu'*; the perfume of garden-grown tomatoes.

There was a sensuality to her foods, a quality that led one to suspect she had slaved over a stove or oven for hours. And yet, those indescribable recipes were simple and "homestyle"-*casareccia*—products that were the fruit of simplicity rather than laborious and intricate activity.

But there was a huge obstacle in duplicating Francesca's culinary endeavors: in all the years we cooked and baked together, I never saw a written recipe of any kind; and she never followed the same process twice. Everything was tailor-made with a "pinch of this" and a "dab of that" being the operative instructions. And these "pinches" and "dabs" varied from time to time depending on her mood, and the availability of the raw ingredients needed.

Years later, when I was left alone to try and remember the ingredients she had used for a specific dish, I realized I had no roadmap. I could vividly recall the smells, textures and tastes of her finished products but had only the vaguest notion on how to achieve the final product. It was like driving a car toward a known destination, having only a vague recollection of the odd road sign or a familiar item en route but without the certainty or comfort of a map.

Some years later, I studied nutrition and, as a result, faced a double obstacle: first, I needed to actually create written recipes that were intelligible strictly from my visual recollections; and second, tweaking them so as to make them "healthy", "light" and "nutritious" . . . and all the while staying true to the wonderful tastes and smells Francesca had created through the generations.

What follows is a small sampling of the recipes I constructed from closely watching Francesca for some three decades, as adapted to the nutritional standards that I learned academically and to the tastes that our modern generation wants and expects. My mother-in-law was a superb cook. She had an innate sense of what would taste delicious. She created foods much like a music composer writes new rhapsodies. There is an innate sense of directionless magic that almost always leads to something comforting and good. Francesca is a tough act to follow and I hope that she is smiling at her daughter-in-law's interpretation of some of the foods that she particularly enjoyed making.

If I may be permitted to put it in the context of Ken's novels, these are foods that I hope are good for the heart and are also nourishment for the soul. I am hopeful that these traditional and yet modern recipes would be among Marco's favorites. In the words of Mark's childhood friend, Luca Moranni, Mark's physical and spiritual travels work up an appetite that can only be satisfied with good food—food that's brimming with simplicity, flavor, sensuality and, of course, tradition.

BUON APPETITO!
Anita Frances Cancellara

LIGHT AND HEALTHY RECIPES FROM MARINA'S KITCHEN

(Marco's Favourites)

Selected recipes of
Anita F. Cancellara, BA, MLS cert. in Advanced Symptomatology, nutrition and Lifestyle Consultant

Zuppe, Antipasti Insalate

[Soups, Appetizers, and Salads]

Pasta E Contorni

[Pasta and Side Dishes]

Carne, Pollo e Pesce

(Meat, Chicken and Fish)

Dolci

Desserts

ZUPPE, ANTIPASTI INSALATE

[SOUPS, APPETIZERS, AND SALADS]

Zuppa Minestrone
[Vegetarian Vegetable Soup]

Delicious on its own, as part of a light vegetarian meal, or as an appetizer, this soup is full of flavourful vegetables. It is nutrient-dense, and vitamin-rich, including vitamins A and K, calcium, iron and fibre. It makes eight appetizer servings or four main course servings. Although the recipe calls for navy beans, it can also be made with romano beans, white kidney beans, or lentils. If desired, it can be prepared with the addition of a small whole wheat pasta such as *tubetti*.

1 cup canned navy or other beans
1 tbsp. olive oil
1 clove garlic, minced
1 medium onion, chopped
1 carrot, chopped
1 rib celery, chopped
1 cup diced tomatoes
4 cups vegetable broth + 1 cup water
½ tsp. salt
¼ tsp. pepper
1 medium potato, cubed, skin on
1 cup green beans, bite-sized pieces
1-3/4 cups cubed, unpeeled zucchini
4 kale leaves, separated from stalks and chopped
¼ cup chopped fresh basil/ 1 tsp. dried
½ tsp. dried oregano
¼ cup chopped fresh parsley
½ cup dry small whole-wheat pasta (optional)
Parmesan Cheese

Rinse, drain and measure beans. Set aside. Chop garlic, onion, carrot and celery in a food processor. In a Dutch oven or large pot, heat oil over medium heat. Add a small amount of the chopped vegetables and bring to a sizzle. Add balance of the chopped vegetables. Turn heat to medium-low, cover the pot and "sweat" the vegetables for ten minutes. Add tomatoes, broth, beans, potatoes, salt and pepper. Stir to mix well and bring to a boil. Reduce heat to low and simmer, partially covered, for ten minutes. Add green beans and tubetti (if using). Cook covered on medium heat for ten minutes. Add zucchini and kale and cook, covered, at medium-low heat for five minutes. Remove from heat and stir in basil, oregano and parsley. Taste and adjust seasoning, if necessary. Ladle into bowls and top each serving with a sprinkling of Parmesan cheese.

Zuppa della Nonna
[Grandma's Turkey Meatball and Orzo Pasta Soup]

This is a lighter version of a family favourite which Nonna used to serve. It's a good source of lean protein. Serves 8.

- 1 lb. lean ground turkey
- 1 egg white, slightly beaten
- 1 tbsp. dried oregano
- 1 tsp. garlic salt
- ¼ cup breadcrumbs
- 2 tbsp. olive oil
- 5 chicken legs (all skin and visible fat removed)
- 6 cups water
- 2 carrots, sliced
- 2 ribs celery, sliced
- 2 green onions, cut in half or ½ cooking onion
- ½ cup parsley, chopped
- ¼ cup dill (or 1 tbsp. dried)
- 1 tbsp. salt (or to taste)
- ½ cup dry orzo, cooked
- Grated Parmesan cheese

MEATBALLS: Combine lean ground turkey with one slightly beaten egg white. Mix in oregano, garlic salt and bread crumbs. Shape into tiny (1/2" in diameter) meatballs. Heat oil at medium-high in a non-stick skillet. Brown meatballs in batches and drain on paper towel. Set aside. (Cooked meatballs can be frozen for up to three months).

SOUP: Place chicken pieces in a Dutch oven or large soup pot and cover with water. Heat to a boil over high heat. As it boils, skim off any scum from the top of the soup until broth is clear. Add the carrots, celery and onion and reduce heat to medium-low. Add the parsley, dill and salt and simmer, gently, for one hour. Skim fat and add more water if needed. Add more salt to taste. When complete, remove the chicken. Cook orzo according to package directions and set aside.

Heat broth on medium-high heat until boiling. Lower heat to medium-low and add meatballs and cooked Orzo. Heat through for about five minutes and serve. Ladle into bowls and top with Parmesan cheese, as desired.

Bruschetta di Pomodoro

This lighter version of a classic Italian appetizer is presented in both the cooked and more rustic uncooked version.

8 slices whole wheat or multigrain baguette
4 cloves garlic, cut in half
2 tbsp. chopped onion
2 tsp. olive oil
2 large vine-ripened tomatoes, diced
Pinch of salt
1 tsp. dried oregano
2 tsp. light Parmesan cheese (optional)

Slice baguette diagonally into eight slices and toast under broiler on both sides until lightly browned. Rub one side of the toasted bread with the cut side of the garlic clove. Heat oil in a skillet over medium-high heat. Add the onion and cook for 3 minutes. Add diced tomato and sprinkle with salt and oregano. Mix well.

Place a rounded tablespoon of tomato mixture on garlic side of toast slices and top with parmesan cheese (if using). Place under the broiler briefly until cheese melts.

As an alternative, top toast slices with a mixture of uncooked tomato, one clove of garlic (minced), oregano, salt and 2 tsp. of olive oil.

Both versions, cooked and uncooked, are equally tasty.

Crostini Di Funghi, Peperoni E Provolone

[mushroom, Red Pepper and Provolone Cheese toasts]

This recipe is my version of the higher calorie Crostini popular in Pisa. It's a great appetizer or as an accompaniment to a hearty minestrone soup.

Crostini can be made with a variety of light and nutritious ingredients. The use of low-fat cheese will retain the taste while lowering calories.

8 medium Cremini mushrooms, sliced
1 red pepper, cut into small cubes
2 tsp. olive oil
4 slices light provolone cheese, in small pieces
¼ tsp. salt
¼ tsp. pepper
½ tsp. dried oregano
¼ tsp. dried basil
8 slices whole wheat baguette
4 garlic cloves, cut in half

Heat olive oil in a skillet over medium-high heat. Add sliced mushrooms and red pepper. Sauté, stirring often, until browned (5 minutes). Mix in salt, pepper, oregano and basil. Combine well. Cover and let stand for a few minutes to soften.

Toast bread slices on one side under broiler. Rub toasted sides with garlic halves. Arrange mushroom/pepper mixture on top of toasted bread slices. Arrange provolone pieces on top of mushroom mixture and put under broiler. Heat until cheese softens. Turn off broiler and leave in oven until cheese melts.

Insalata Capresona
["salad from Capri" in campania]

This light, nutrient-rich salad (filled with calcium, lycopene and delicate leafy greens) is great on its own for lunch or as an appetizer. Italian Bocconcini ("little bites") are a light, fresh type of mozzarella cheese and can be found at deli counters or supermarkets in plastic tubs filled with liquid containing whey and/or water.

Makes four appetizer portions or three lunch servings.

3 cups organic baby greens
3 large vine-ripened tomatoes
12 fresh basil leaves
1 tbsp. olive oil
¼ cup balsamic vinegar
¼ tsp. salt
1/8 tsp. pepper
4 medium-sized balls Bocconcini cheese

Cover the bottom of a large platter with a layer of baby greens. Cut each tomato into four slices and arrange on the bed of greens. Cut each bocconcino into three slices and place one slice on top of each tomato slice. Top each bocconcini slice with a basil leaf.

In a measuring cup mix the balsamic vinegar, olive oil, salt and pepper with a fork. Drizzle over the salad and serve.

This salad can be prepared and kept covered in the refrigerator until ready to serve. Drizzle with balsamic mixture before serving.

Insalata Di Arancia E Finocchio
[Orange and Fennel Salad]

Raw fennel is crunchy like celery but has a sweet liquorice flavour. This dish is Sicilian in origin. The salad is very light and low in calories, and provides a good source of vitamin C and fibre. (Serves 4)

2 large navel oranges
1 small bulb fennel, diced
¼ tsp. red pepper flakes
2 tsp. olive oil
¼ tsp. salt (or to taste)
Shaved Asiago cheese

Peel and cut the orange into small chunks and place in a large salad bowl. Mix in the sliced fennel and sprinkle with red pepper flakes. Drizzle with the olive oil and season with salt. Shave a block of Asiago cheese with a potato peeler and add to salad.

This salad is delicious served with slices of rustic Italian bread that has been lightly brushed with olive oil and toasted under the broiler until well-browned.

Insalata Casareccia di Pomodoro
[homestyle tomato salad]

This cool, refreshing summer salad is a tasty treat. Add an ice cube for an extra chill. (Serves 4)

3 medium vine-ripened tomatoes cut into chunks
2 stalks of celery, sliced
½ medium English cucumber, cut into chunks
4 green onions (tips removed) stems only
2 tsp. olive oil
2 tsp. oregano
Salt, to taste
Water to cover
Ice cubes (optional)
Whole wheat baguette (optional)

In a large bowl, mix the tomato, celery slices and cucumber chunks together. Sprinkle with oregano and salt. Stir to combine. Divide the mixture between four soup bowls. Add the chopped green onion to each bowl and drizzle with ½ tsp. of olive oil. Add cold water to just cover the vegetables. Add an ice cube for a cool treat. A whole wheat baguette, torn into bite-sized pieces, can be added for rustic flavour and texture.

Insalata Di Ceci
[Chickpea Salad]

Chickpeas are a very good source of folic acid, fibre, and manganese. They are also a good source of protein and minerals such as iron, copper, zinc, and magnesium.

A tasty healthy option, this Chickpea Salad goes well with baked Cannelloni (see recipe p.15). Serves 4.

1 can chickpeas, rinsed and drained
2 tbsp. diced red onion
1 small green pepper, diced
1 small red pepper, diced
1 clove garlic, minced
½ tsp. dried oregano
¼ tsp. dried thyme
2 tbsp. chopped fresh basil
2 tbsp. chopped fresh parsley
2 tbsp. olive oil
¼ cup red wine vinegar
½ tsp. salt
¼ tsp. pepper
4 large lettuce leaves

In a large bowl combine chickpeas, red onion, peppers, garlic, oregano, thyme, basil and parsley. In a small measuring cup whisk together olive oil, red wine vinegar, salt and pepper. Pour over chickpea mixture and toss gently to combine. Serve on a chilled lettuce leaf.

Pasta E Contorni

[Pasta and Side Dishes]

Spaghetti Alla Puttanesca

A favourite dish that boasts both great flavours and healthy ingredients, with Omega-3s and lycopene topping the list.

Prepare this delicious pasta and sauce to delight guests on special occasions or as an everyday treat. (Serves 4)

1 Tbsp. olive oil
4 tsp. minced garlic (about 4 cloves)
½ cup Italian parsley, chopped
¼ cup capers
½ cup pitted black olives, chopped
4 anchovies, chopped
¼ tsp. chili pepper flakes
2 tsp. dried oregano
1 can diced tomatoes (796 ml/28 fl.ounces)
1-1/2 cups chopped arugula
375g. whole wheat spaghetti
Light Parmesan cheese (optional)

In a large, deep skillet over medium-high heat, sauté garlic in olive oil for one minute. Add the Italian parsley, capers, olives, anchovies, chilli pepper flakes and oregano. Stir well and cook for two minutes. Add tomatoes and simmer (at medium-low heat) for 35 minutes, stirring occasionally. Add the arugula and simmer for another minute. Remove from heat.

Cook pasta as directed on the package, drain and add to the skillet. Over medium heat, let the pasta warm in the sauce, stirring occasionally to blend all the flavours. Simmer for two minutes more. Transfer to a large serving bowl or platter and pass the Parmesan cheese. A warmed sliced whole wheat or multigrain baguette will complete this tasty meal.

Melanzane Alla Parmigiana
[Eggplant Parmesan]

Although not a "pasta" dish per se, this lighter version of the classic recipe involves baking, not frying, the eggplant slices thus retaining the wonderful flavour while eliminating many of the calories. A fresh green salad completes the meal. (Serves 3)

1 Tbsp. olive oil
1 jar tomato passata (strained, crushed tomatoes)
1 can diced tomatoes (400 ml/14 oz.)
1 clove garlic
¼ cup chopped fresh basil
1 tsp. dried oregano
1 tsp. dried basil
¼ tsp. salt
Olive oil cooking spray
3 egg whites
3 tbsp. water
2 medium eggplants, sliced into 18, ¼" slices
1-1/4 cups breadcrumbs
2 tbsp. olive oil
1-1/4 cup grated part-skim mozzarella or light 4-cheese Italiano blend
½ cup grated Parmesan cheese

TOMATO SAUCE: In a large pot or Dutch oven, sauté minced garlic in oil at medium-low heat for three minutes. Add passata, diced tomatoes, basil and spices and bring to a boil. Reduce heat and simmer for 20 minutes.

EGGPLANT: Spray two non-stick baking sheets with cooking spray. Beat egg whites and water until foamy. Dip the eggplant slices into the egg whites and then into the breadcrumbs. Place on the prepared baking sheets and drizzle with the olive oil. Bake 30-40 minutes until nicely browned at 400°F.

ASSEMBLY: Ladle one cup of tomato sauce into the bottom of a 9 x 13" baking dish. Layer six of the eggplant slices, lightly cover with more tomato sauce, then the mozzarella and parmesan cheeses. Repeat for two more layers spreading the tomato sauce to edge of each layer, and ending with the cheeses.

Bake uncovered at 400° F for 25 minutes. Remove from oven, cover with foil and keep warm until ready to serve.

Cannelloni Al Formaggio
[Cheese-filled Cannelloni Pasta]

Light and nutritious, this recipe is a good source of calcium. Serve with protein-rich Chick Pea Salad (see recipe p.8) for a quick and tasty meal. (Serves 3)

18 cannelloni shells
1 tbsp. olive oil
1 clove garlic, minced
1 jar tomato passata
1 can diced tomatoes (400 ml/14 oz.)
¼ cup chopped fresh basil or 1 tsp. dried
1 tsp. dried oregano
¼ tsp. salt
1 green onion, chopped
2 tbsp. parsley, chopped
1 container light Ricotta cheese
3 tbsp. skim milk
¼ cup part-skim mozzarella cheese
¼ cup light Parmesan cheese

TOMATO SAUCE: In a large pot or Dutch oven, sauté minced garlic in oil at medium-low heat for three minutes. Add passata, diced tomatoes, basil and spices and bring to a boil. Reduce heat and simmer for 20 minutes.

Cook cannelloni as per package directions. Rinse and set aside.

FILLING: In a large mixing bowl combine ricotta cheese, green onion, parsley, milk, mozzarella cheese and Parmesan cheese. Mix well until smooth. Slice open each cannelloni shell, fill with ricotta mixture and roll up.

ASSEMBLY: Ladle a cup of tomato sauce onto the bottom of a 9" x 13" baking dish. Arrange cannelloni, seam side down, over the sauce in a single layer. Pour sauce over the top of the cannelloni. Sprinkle with two tablespoons Parmesan cheese. Cover and bake for about 40 minutes at 350° F. until hot and bubbly.

NOTE: If using oven-ready cannelloni shells, fill and assemble as above, and bake following package directions.

Lasagna con Spinachi e Funghi
[Lasagna with Spinach and Mushrooms]

This is a light vegetarian version of lasagna with red peppers and mushrooms in a rich tomato sauce. (Serves 4)

1 Tbsp. oilive oil
1 medium onion, diced
2 cloves garlic, minced
8 oz. cremini mushrooms, sliced
2 cups baby spinach chopped
28 oz. can diced tomatoes
1 cup tomato passata
1 tbsp. dried oregano
½ tsp. salt
¼ cup fresh basil, chopped (or ½ tsp. dried)
¼ cup Italian parsley, chopped
9 whole wheat lasagna noodles
1-1/4 cup part-skim mozzarella cheese
½ cup light Parmesan cheese

VEGETABLE/TOMATO SAUCE: Heat the olive oil in a large saucepan or Dutch oven on medium-low heat. Add the onion and garlic and "sweat" the vegetables covered for three minutes. Turn heat to medium-high, add mushrooms and sauté, stirring occasionally for four minutes. Add the tomatoes, spinach, passata, oregano, salt, basil and parsley. Stir well and bring to a boil. Reduce heat to medium-low and simmer sauce for twenty minutes, stirring occasionally.

NOODLES: Cook lasagne noodles according to package directions and rinse with cool water. Set aside.

ASSEMBLY: Cover the bottom of a 9" x 13" baking dish with one cup of sauce. Place three lasagna noodles, side-by-side lengthwise over the sauce. Top with more sauce then mozzarella cheese and sprinkle with Parmesan cheese. Repeat lawyers twice, ending with vegetable sauce and cheeses. Distribute leftover sauce at the sides of lasagne in the baking dish.

Cover with foil and bake at 350° F. for 40 minutes. After removing from the oven, let the lasagne rest, covered, at least 15 minutes before serving.

CONTORNO DI RAPINI
[SIDE DISH OF SAUTEED RAPINI]

1 bunch rapini
1 tbsp. olive oil
1 tsp. crushed garlic
¼ tsp. cayenne pepper
¼ tsp. hot pepper flakes
Salt to taste

PREPARE RAPINI: Place the rapini in fresh water, rinse and drain.

BLANCH [helps to eliminate some of the bitter taste]: Place the rapini in a large pot of rapidly boiling water for five minutes. Drain in a colander and rinse with cold water to stop cooking and preserve colour. Set aside.

SAUTE: In a non-stick frying pan on medium-high heat, sauté crushed garlic in oil, for one minute. Add rapini and stir to distribute garlic and oil into rapini. Sprinkle with cayenne pepper and hot pepper flakes and mix well. Add salt to taste. Remove from heat and allow to rest to blend flavours. Serve warmed or at room temperature.

Patatine Rosse All'Arroste
[Roasted Baby Red Potatoes]

Red potatoes a popular Italian side dish. Roasted red potatoes are high in several key nutrients. One 4 oz. serving provides at least 8% of thiamin, niacin, vitamins B6 and C, copper, iron, manganese, magnesium and potassium. In addition, using olive oil contributes heart-healthy omega-3 fatty acids. (Serves 4)

20 baby red potatoes, cut in half
1 tbsp. olive oil
1 tbsp. dried rosemary
1 tsp. salt
½ tsp. freshly ground pepper

Preheat oven to 450° F. In a large bowl, toss the potatoes with the oil, rosemary, salt and pepper.

Spray a large baking sheet with olive oil cooking spray. Put potatoes in a single layer, cut sides down and roast for 25 minutes, stirring once after 15 minutes, until lightly browned.

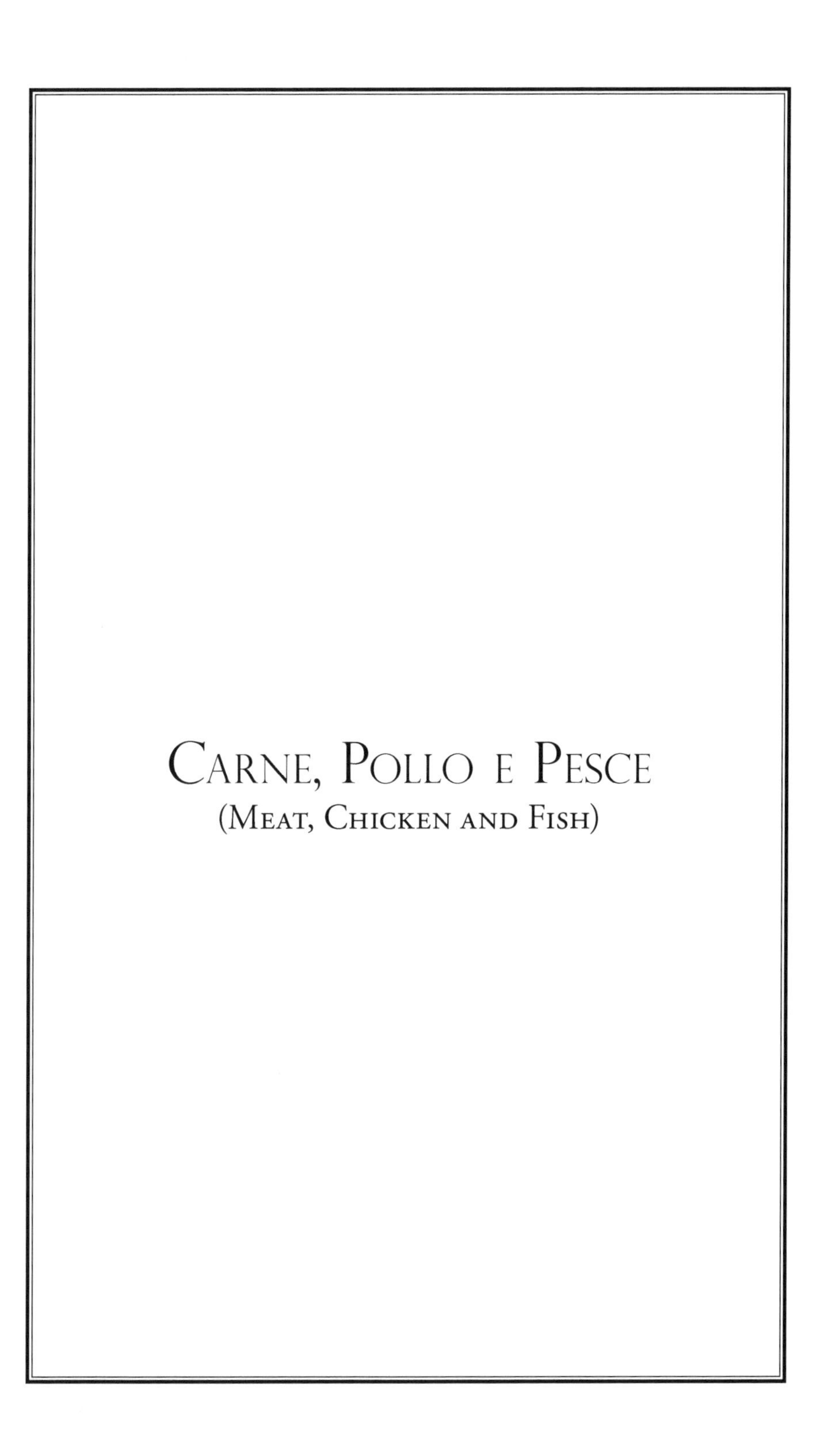

Carne, Pollo e Pesce
(Meat, Chicken and Fish)

Pollo alla Bolognese
[chicken in bolognese Sauce]

This family favourite is reminiscent of a fantastic meal I enjoyed at a restaurant in the "*Mecrato dei Fiori*" in Rome. It is a lighter version of the classic using whole wheat pappardelle noodles and ground chicken but it retains the richness and flavour of this hearty dish. (Serves 4)

- 350 g. whole wheat pappardelle noodles
- 2 tbsp. olive oil
- 1 lb. lean ground chicken
- 1 tsp. salt
- 2 carrots, diced
- 2 stalks celery, diced
- 1 clove garlic, minced
- 1 large onion, diced
- 28 oz. can crushed tomatoes
- ¼ cup parsley, chopped
- 1 tsp. dried oregano
- 1 tsp. dried basil
- ¼ tsp. black pepper

Heat 1 tbsp. olive oil in a dutch oven over medium-high heat. Add the ground chicken, breaking up into small pieces using a large cooking spoon as it cooks. Sprinkle ½ tsp. salt over the chicken. Once cooked through remove to a bowl. Drain any liquid from the skillet, add 1 tbsp. oil and cook carrots, celery, onion and garlic, covered until lightly browned (approximately 8 minutes). Add tomatoes, parsley, oregano, basil, pepper and remaining ½ tsp. salt and ½ cup water. Bring to a boil, reduce heat and simmer, covered, for 12 minutes, stirring occasionally and adding water when necessary. Stir in reserved chicken and juices and simmer covered for 3 minutes.

Cook pappardelle in salted water (1/2 tsp. salt) timed according to package directions, and drain. Add to simmering sauce and mix well. Transfer to a large bowl or platter and serve.

Polpettine e Spaghetti

[Spaghetti and mini meatballs]

This is a light and healthy version of spaghetti and meatballs which appeals to the whole family. I have used lean ground chicken for the meatballs, but lean ground turkey, veal or beef can be substituted. (Serves 4)

1 lb. lean ground chicken
1 egg white
2 tbsp. oregano
1 tbsp. garlic salt
¼ cup breadcrumbs
2 tbsp. Parmesan cheese
350 g. whole wheat spaghetti
½ tsp. salt
¼ tsp. hot chili pepper flakes (optional)

1 tbsp. olive oil
1 medium onion, diced
2 cloves garlic, minced
28 oz. can diced tomatoes
1 cup crushed tomatoes
¼ cup parsley, chopped
¼ cup basil, chopped
1 tsp. dried oregano

Preheat oven to 350°F.

MEATBALLS: In a large bowl, combine ground chicken with the breadcrumbs, Parmesan cheese, oregano, garlic salt and egg white. Mix well. Using a tablespoon take sufficient meat to roll into 2" diameter meatballs. Place meatballs in rows on a large baking sheet that has been lined with parchment paper. Bake for 20 minutes.

SAUCE: In a large Dutch oven over medium heat, sauté garlic and onion then cover and let "sweat" for 3 minutes. Add diced tomatoes and crushed tomatoes, parsley, basil, oregano, pepper flakes (if using), and salt. Bring to a boil, lower heat and simmer for 20 minutes stirring occasionally.

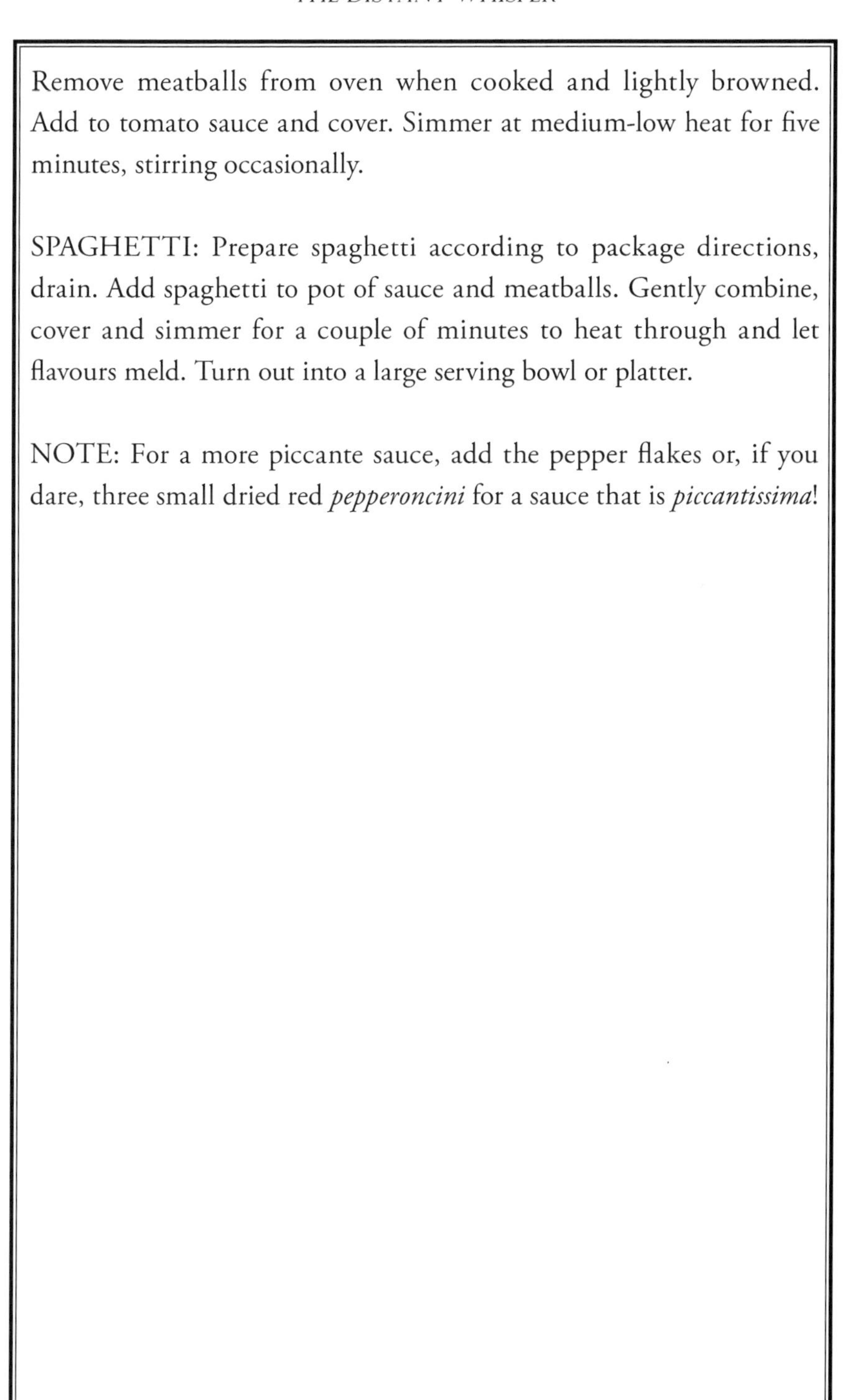

Remove meatballs from oven when cooked and lightly browned. Add to tomato sauce and cover. Simmer at medium-low heat for five minutes, stirring occasionally.

SPAGHETTI: Prepare spaghetti according to package directions, drain. Add spaghetti to pot of sauce and meatballs. Gently combine, cover and simmer for a couple of minutes to heat through and let flavours meld. Turn out into a large serving bowl or platter.

NOTE: For a more piccante sauce, add the pepper flakes or, if you dare, three small dried red *pepperoncini* for a sauce that is *piccantissima*!

Cotoletta alla Milanese
[Breaded Veal Cutlets]

This lighter version of the popular dish is baked, not fried in oil. Chicken or turkey cutlets can also be used in place of the veal. (Serves 4)

4 medium-sized veal, chicken or turkey cutlets
½ cup Kellogg's cornflake crumbs
½ heaping cup of bread crumbs
2 egg whites, beaten
¼ tsp. dried basil
¼ tsp. dried oregano
¼ tsp. salt
2 tbsp. olive oil

Preheat oven to 400° F. Spray a large baking sheet with olive oil cooking spray and spread evenly over the baking sheet using a paper towel.

Prepare the cutlets by placing the meat between two pieces of waxed paper and pounding with a meat mallet or the back of a small skillet until thin. Lightly beat the egg whites and set aside. Combine the cornflake crumbs, breadcrumbs and spices on a large plate.

Place the prepared baking sheet into the oven for one minute.

Dip the cutlets, one at a time, into the egg white and then the crumb mixture and coat thoroughly. Place the breaded cutlets onto the prepared baking sheet in a single layer. Drizzle with some of the olive oil and bake for seven minutes. Turn the meat over and bake for another seven minutes or longer until cutlets are nicely browned.

The cutlets can be served on their own, along with a lemon wedge, in the authentic style, or accompanied by a "*contorno*" (side dish) of sautéed Rapini and garlic (see recipe p. 14].

Pollo alla Cacciatore
[Hunter's Chicken]

A popular dish which provides an excellent source of protein, lycopene and Vitamin A is delicious served on its own with a crusty loaf of Italian bread or with a side dish of whole wheat penne. (Serves 4)

2 tbsp. olive oil
11 or 12 chicken thighs (bone-in)
½ onion, chopped
2 clove garlic, minced
8 oz. cremini mushrooms, (10) sliced
1 large red pepper, diced
1 jar Passata or 1-28 oz can crushed tomatoes
¼ cup red cooking wine
2 tbsp. parsley, chopped
2 tbsp. basil, chopped (or ½ tsp. dried)
1 tsp. salt
½ tsp. black pepper
200 g. whole wheat penne pasta
1 cup diced tomatoes

Remove skin and all visible fat from chicken pieces. Heat 1 tbsp. olive oil in a large, deep non-stick skillet on medium-high heat. Add chicken and brown on all sides. Remove from skillet and set aside.

Wipe out skillet with a paper towel. Add the remaining 1 tbsp. oil to skillet and add onion and garlic. Cover skillet and "sweat" contents for three minutes. Add the mushroom slices and raise heat to medium-high. Cook, stirring occasionally for three minutes. Add the diced red pepper and cook, covered, at medium for five minutes. Add the tomato passata, diced tomatoes, wine, parsley, basil, salt and pepper, bring to a boil.

Add reserved chicken and ½ cup water. Stir well to combine. Reduce heat to medium-low and cook, covered, for 45 minutes, stirring occasionally, adding water when necessary if sauce thickens too quickly.

Turn the chicken and sauce out onto a large serving bowl or platter reserving some sauce in the skillet. Prepare penne (if using) according to package directions. Drain, rinse and add to skillet. Pour into bowl and serve.

Zuppa Di Pesce
[Italian Fish Stew]

This makes a light, vitamin and mineral-rich, heart-healthy meal that is high in Vitamin B12, zinc, magnesium and potassium. It is best prepared with fresh seafood bought the same day as it is cooked. Salad greens tossed with light olive oil, red wine vinegar and sea salt will compliment this tasty stew. (Serves 2-3)

1 tbsp. olive oil
1 medium onion, diced
2 cloves garlic, minced
¼ tsp. red pepper flakes
28 oz. can diced tomatoes
¼ cup tomato Passata
4 tbsp. chopped parsley
½ cup dry white wine
1 bay leaf
¼ tsp. salt
18 mussels
1 calamari, cut in rings
1 large filet of cod (7 oz.) cut in 3" pieces
Toasted baguette slices

In a large, deep skillet, heat oil over medium heat. Add onion, garlic and red pepper flakes and cook covered until softened (about five minutes). Add tomatoes, tomato passata, wine, bay leaf and salt. Simmer, covered, over medium-low heat for 10 minutes. Taste and add additional salt if needed. Add cod and cook for one minute at medium heat. Add the mussels and calamari and cook, covered, for six minutes. Spoon some sauce over the mussels. Gently ladle into large soup bowls and sprinkle with parsley.

Slice baguette into slices; brush lightly with olive oil and place under the broiler until toasted. Serve on the sides of the bowls filled with the zuppa di pesce.

Baccalà alla Salsa di Pomodoro
[Cod in Tomato Sauce]

This recipe calls for salt cod which must be pre-soaked to remove much of the salt while retaining its unique flavour. It is delicious served over a small pasta such as *penne rigate*. The fish is a good source of light protein. (Serves 4)

2 large pieces of salt cod
1 tbsp. olive oil
2 cloves garlic, chopped
2 tbsp. parsley, chopped
10 cremini mushrooms, sliced
1 red pepper, diced
1 can San Marzano tomatoes, chopped

PREPARE FISH: Cut the salt cod into 4 pieces and place in a large bowl. Cover with cold water. Cover and soak for 8 hours; rinse and recover with fresh water. Repeat every 8 hours for 2 ½ days. Cut into serving-size pieces (about 4" in length).

SAUCE: In a large, deep skillet, heat the olive oil over medium heat. Add the onion and garlic, turn the heat to medim-low and "sweat" covered for three minutes. Add the mushrooms and brown slightly. Add the red peppers and soften (four minutes). Add the chopped tomatoes and parsley. Add the cod pieces and combine. Simmer on medium-low heat for 25-30 minutes or until the sauce thickens.

Serve with pasta, roasted baby red potatoes (see p. 15) or tossed salad.

Dolci

Desserts

Pastiz Della Nonna
[Grandma's Cheesecake]

This is a lighter version of the family favourite which eliminates the high-calorie crust and substitutes low-fat dairy to retain the distinctly delicious flavour. Rich in calcium and protein, the addition of raisins provides a tasty iron-rich surprise for added flavour Mangia bene!

¼ tsp. cinnamon
1-1/4 cups graham cracker crumbs
3 tbsp. margarine or butter melted
1-1/2 x 475 g. tubs light 5% MF ricotta cheese
¾ cup sugar
3 eggs
1 tsp. vanilla
½ cup plain fat-free yogurt
½ cup raisins
2 tbsp. flour

Preheat oven to 350° F. Grease the sides and bottom of a 9" spring form pan.

Place the raisins in a small bowl, and top with just enough hot water to cover. Allow to soften (10 minutes). When soft to the touch, pour off water. Set aside.

CRUST: Combine the graham cracker crumbs and cinnamon in a mixing bowl. Add the melted butter and toss with fork until combined. Press the crumb mixture into the bottom of the prepared spring form pan. Set aside.

FILLING: In a large bowl, thoroughly combine the ricotta cheese and sugar. Add the eggs and mix well. Stir in yogurt and vanilla. Add the softened raisins, blending thoroughly. Mix in the flour. Blend well. Pour over crust in spring form pan.

Bake for 45 minutes in the centre of the oven until done (the cheesecake will still jiggle slightly in the middle). Remove from oven, let cool and then refrigerate.

To serve, release and remove the sides of the spring form, leaving the cake resting on the bottom of the pan. Enjoy a slice (or two) with your favourite beverage—Nonna always liked her pastiz with a cup of tea and lemon.

AMARETTI
[ALMOND COOKIES]

This high-fibre, high protein and low calorie cookie has no added fat and only two tablespoons of flour. They're great with an espresso or cappuccino after a meal or as a light snack. One of my most requested recipes—makes about 45-50 cookies.

1-7/8 cups whole raw almonds
7/8 cup sugar
2 tablespoons flour
1/8 tsp. salt
4 egg whites
½ tsp. vanilla
1 tsp. almond extract

ALMONDS: Spread the almonds in a single layer on a baking sheet and toast in a 300° F oven for eight minutes. Remove from oven and place on a platter in the fridge to cool. When the almonds are no longer warm to the touch (30 minutes) pour into a food processor.

DOUGH: To almonds in the food processor add the sugar, flour and salt. Pulse just until almond mixture is finely ground [careful not to over-process]. Remove to a large bowl. Beat the egg whites in a small bowl until foamy and add to the ground almond mixture—do not mix—add vanilla and almond extract and then lightly stir everything together being careful not to over-mix.

Line two large baking sheets with parchment paper. Using two teaspoons, form the mixture into small balls, dropping in rows on the baking sheets.

Bake each sheet individually in the centre of a 300° F oven for 25 minutes. Remove from oven and transfer cookies still on the parchment paper to a cooling rack for 20 minutes.

Store cookies in a covered container to retain freshness. These cookies can keep for a few weeks, but should disappear before then.

Granita di caffè
[Coffee sorbet]

Reminiscent of lazy summer afternoons in Italy, this frozen dessert is very low in calories. Similar to sorbet, is a refreshing finish to a spicy meal or simply on its own. Made with decaffeinated or regular coffee, Makes approximately 8 servings.

1 cup espresso or strong brewed coffee (decaf or regular)
2 cups water
½ cup sugar
1 tsp. vanilla

SUGAR SYRUP: Put 1 cup of water in a saucepan, add sugar and stir with a fork to combine. Heat over medium-high two minutes or until sugar has melted. Transfer to a mixing bowl and cover loosely with a piece of foil. Refrigerate until completely cool (2-1/2 hours).

When cooled, add remaining cup of water, espresso (or coffee you are using) and vanilla. Blend well. Pour mixture into a 9" x 13" metal baking pan and place in freezer for approximately three hours. As it freezes, stir with a fork every 20 minutes, scraping the ice as it forms on the sides of the pan, and at the same time scooping and stirring the mixture. The finished product will resemble icy slush when done.

Another easy and delicious coffee-based dessert is *Affogato*: Place a scoop of mild-flavoured gelato (such as "*torrone*") in a wide shallow glass or dessert dish and pour over it a single or double espresso (can be decaffeinated).